LETTERS FROM CHICKPEA

Letters
From
Chickpea

Edward G. Klemm, Jr.

FITHIAN PRESS · SANTA BARBARA · 1990

Design and typography by Jim Cook/Santa Barbara

Published by Fithian Press
Post Office Box 1525
Santa Barbara, California 93120

LIBRARY OF CONGRESS CATALOGING-IN-PUBLICATION DATA

Klemm, Edward G., 1910-
    Letters from Chickpea / Edward G. Klemm, Jr.
    ISBN 0-931832-49-7: $8.95
    I. Title.
PS3561.L386L48   1990   90-2780
813.'.54—dc20   CIP

To all small towns and
the people who make them so special.

Letters From Chickpea

1.

Chickpea
U.S.A.

Dear Cousin Elrod:

I enjoy your visit very much an' hope you arrive safe back in Chicago. There is not much news to write. In a small town like Chickpea you don't see very much, but the gossip make up for it.

Miss Cranbock who run the Diner restaurant nearly went bankruptured givin' too much credit. She had more dead beats for customers than she had plain beets in her vegetables. When she quits givin' credit the folks at Caney Church gets mad and some of them quits eatin' there. But Miss Cranbock say she don't see Caney Church takin' no IOUs in their collection box.

You remember me interducin' you to Doc Storkbill the time I gets the stomach ache? Well, his practice done fell off considerable since his son open a funeral parlor.

The governorial election is heatin' up. One of them candydates from the State Capital was braggin' on himself so much I tole him I'd vote for him if he was runnin' for God. All them candydates talks the same. All they wants is to spend our money. They says we needs better roads, better police protection and better schools. I thinks all we needs is better politicians. But from what I hears they is all dead.

Jethro Crump come back from Chicago right after you leaves an' tole us about eatin' in one of them fancy restaurants you all got up there. He say the menu is in a foreign language and he can't read it so he lets his uncle do the orderin'. He tole us they brung him a dish call a salat which is nothing but green stuff like he feed his cattle.

Then they brung him something call a lobster. He was afraid to eat it at first but when he try it it taste pretty good. An' then Arnold Dinglehoffer ask Jethro what a lobster was and Jethro low it was some kind of a bug what live in the ocean.

It seem for years the population of Chickpea has been 1,199. We can't seem to get our goal of 1,200. Now we're waitin' for Mrs. Bramliff to have her baby. Miss Cranbock say wouldn't it be nice if she had twins so we'd top 1,200?

That drought that was goin' on while you was here was broke t'other day by a tornado which broke a lot of other things too. I heared one farmer was milkin' his cow when the tornado hit right over his head and carried off his cow leavin' him holdin' the bag.

Yesterday was a black day for Chickpea. The Blakemores moves away an' we lose seven people out of our population. It don't look like we'll ever get to 1,200. Stew Borders say if we get any smaller we'll lose our zip code. Miss Cranbock is now sayin' she hope Mrs. Bramliff has quintripulets.

That's all the news for now.

Cousin Hank

2.

Chickpea
U.S.A.

Dear Cousin Elrod:

We had some real excitement here in Chickpea t'other day. Some city feller was drivin' through an' he knock Rubin, the village idiot, down on Main Street. He look back at Rubin lyin' in the street an yell, "Look out!" Rubin raise up an' call out, "What for? You comin' back?" So I guess Rubin ain't quite the idiot we thinks he is.

Jason Gump's wife leave him for another man an' he get all broke up. He runs his car in a ditch, an' fall down the steps of his porch an' break his arm. That night his feed store burn. If it weren't for bad luck he wouldn't have no luck at all.

There's been talk of improvin' the Good Samaritan Hospital on the edge of town. It seem everybody's in favor of it except Gilmore, the undertaker. This has hurt his business worse than when he buy a new hearse an' go around sayin' everybody was dyin' to ride in it.

West Bennet has rent out the back room of his Cracker Barrel General Store to the U.S. Post Office to sell stamps and pick up parcels. Now he's goin' around tellin' everybody he own the Federal Building in Chickpea.

Somethin's got to be done about educatin' our kids. I asks Willie Maddox if they has a dictionary I could borrow an' he say, "A what? Do you mean the Holy Bible?"

The reason I wants this dictionary book was on account of we once had a feller in Chickpea who was so smart they call him Pluto. A man from the city tole me t'other day they must of mean Plato and I wants that dictionary to see if he was right and, by gosh, he was right.

I finally had to go buy me one of them dictionaries. But I'm glad I did cause you can learn a lot. I found out Pluto was some sort of a god who lives a long time ago and I also learn philosopher ain't spelt with a f.

One thing that Plato feller in Chickpea say was "the best way to remember somethin' is not to forget it." I always remember that.

Lum Keller, the bootlegger get careless an' get himself arrested last January. The prosicutin' attorney make the mistake of keepin' the evidence in the basement of the court house where there ain't no heat an' it froze solit. The judge throw the case out sayin' if there ain't enough alcohol in Lum's moonshine to keep it from freezin' it can't be illegal. He recommend they retry Lum on defrawdin' the public.

Caney Church has got some new competition. A Sister Kaye has start preachin' on a vacant lot in town an' is goin' over big with the ladies in Chickpea. She's got them talkin' in tongues and givin' her their money. It's drivin' most of their husbands to drink and Jerry who run the Lion's Den Saloon is makin' as much out of Sister Kaye's preachin' as she is. In fack, he say she is the best thing that happen since prohibition was repeal.

Bill Johnson—he's the rich feller on Mason Street—buys one of them tellyvision sets when they first come out and everbody start comin' over to help him watch it. It get so bad he buys him another set an' puts it on the front porch next to his wife's washin' machine so folks could watch it from his front yard. This work for a while but finally a near riot break out over what they wants to watch and they steps all over his begonias. So Bill just take the set back in the house and lock his door.

Jake Staples come near leavin' his wife. He come home from the dentist an' tole her the dentist is real up-to-date an' has got a vacuum he put in your mouth to clean it out an'she say, "Why didn't he use that vacuum you already got in your head?"

Pat Wilburn, that feller I interduces you to when you was visitin' me, had to go in the Good Samaritan Hospital for a operation an' I went to see him before they operates on him an' I asked him if there is anything I can get him an' he say, "Get somebody to take my place."

I was over to Tink Collin's house t'other day to get some of his wife's eggs—I mean her chickins' eggs—an' I see he got three holes cut in the bottom of his back door. I asks him why he got these three holes in the bottom of his door for an' he tole me he got three cats an' when he say scat he mean scat.

On my way home I stops by Stew Borders place an' he is all rile up with his wife. He ask me if I ever heared of the law of supply an' demand. An' when I says I have he tole me he is gettin' tired of supplyin' the money an' his wife demandin' it. He go on to say she got a terrible memory that just about drive him crazy—she don't never forget nothin'.

Miss Cranbock got her a waitress down at her diner what is real mean an' nasty like an' I asks her why she don't fire her. Miss Cranbock say she don't fire her 'cause when she wait on them out-of-town salesmen what eat there an' is usually homesick it make them feel at home.

That's all the news for now.

Cousin Hank

3.

Chickpea
U.S.A.

Dear Cousin Elrod:

We was talkin' t'other day down at the Cracker Barrel Gen. Store about how is the best way to enjoy corn. Some say they likes to eat it on the cob, but they is the ones with teeth. I low I likes corn pudding best. Stew Borders say he like to drink it, which is the first sensible thing I ever hear him say.

Ever since Jim an' Neva Cramer get a divorce she has been cryin' an' carryin' on somethin' awful. Everbody say she's takin' losin' her husband real hard, but Miss Pinwhistle say what break Neva up is if Jim had of die she would have got his insurance. This way he's a total loss.

Miss Thornberry can't get over eddycation even after bein' retire from school teachin' for ten years. She take some of them intellectual magazines that come out of places like New York an' is always tellin' people about what she reads in them. Yesterday she was tellin' everbody about a articule on a scientist name of Darwin who say man come from monkeys an' if you ever been to Chickpea you will know he must be right. Stew Borders low this Darwin feller must be right, too, 'cause some people he know don't look like they come far enough. An' Mr. Jamison say if monkeys could read, that article would make them mad.

They was talkin' about music down at the Cracker Barrel Gen. Store t'other day an' Leviticus Gilmore low there is a music instrument call a zylophone an' none of us believes him. When I gets home I looks it up in my dictionary book an' either there ain't no such instrument or my dictionary ain't no good. I looks all through the z's a dozen times an' never finds it. There ain't many z's in my dictionary so I knows I didn't miss it.

Did I ever tell you old Doc Storkbill has been coroner for about a year? He tole me the hardest case he ever have is when Henry Estes' father die. He say the old man did nothin' but set in a chair all day an' sleep so it was hard to tell if he was dead or not. Henry ask if they could bury the old man settin' in a chair as that was the way they remembers him. I met Lum Keller, the bootlegger, at the funeral parlor when I paid my repecks to old man Estes. I think Lum is the only one who know why the old man set around all day without movin'. Lum say he goes night an' day himself 'cause sleepin' is one thing you can do after you is dead.

Glave Richards come back from Central City all rile up. He say he go to one of them art fairs an' see so-call artists gettin' thousands of dollars for puttin' a little paint on a piece of paper an' he can't get two-hunerd dollars puttin' a lot of paint on a big house.

I wish I could have knowed that Plato feller I writ you about before. My daddy tole me he ask Plato one day why we is here an' Plato say we is here to help others. I wish I could of ask him what the others is here for, 'cause my daddy couldn't tell me when I ask him.

Stew Borders was mad yesterday. He told me he was at a supermarket in a maul an' it taken him a hour to find the instant coffee.

Elrod, I was gettin' ready to throw my dictionary away when I asks Miss Thornberry if there is such a contraption as a zylophone an' she tole me there is an' that it's spelt with a x. Now ain't that the silliest thing you ever hear of? Anyway I looks in the x's an' there it is. One thing about Miss Thornberry is she don't tell no lies an' that is probably why she ain't rich or ever get married.

If there is two sides to a question that Stew Borders always pick the wrong one. Somebody say about him there is no fool like a old fool which just go to show how experience help. I met Stew t'other day an' he look real down an' I asks him what is the matter an' he say he been talkin' to Rev Tatum who fuss at him an' tell him if God was to go fishin' an' catch him He would throw him back. Later on I meet Rev. Tatum an' he get to talkin' about that fake preacher, Sister Kaye, who is doin' so well when it come to collectin' money. He say he heared her tellin' her members you can't take it with you but she is takin' it from them. I figgers out the reason you can't take it with you is 'cause preachers like this Sister Kaye gets it from you before you goes.

That's all the news for now.

Cousin Hank

4.

Chickpea
U.S.A.

Dear Cousin Elrod:

Chickpea done got trouble an' don't know it. Mr. Jamison's son, Craig, graduate from college an' is helpin' his Dad run the hardware store until he find somethin' better to do. Well it turn out he think he's a philosopher like that Plato feller what live here years ago. It's got so you can't go in the store to buy some nails without Craig is always tellin' you what some feller by the name of Confusion who live somewhere in China say or what some Greek with a name like Aristopholes say. Craig tole me he is tryin' to model his life after these fellers an' that he has already come up with a thought of his own. Of course, I knows he want me to ask him what it is so I asks him what it is an' he show me a empty box an' tole me it contain the most valuable thing there is an' when I tole him it look empty to me he laugh an' say I ain't thinkin'. If he know what I is thinkin' he would of get mad so I don't say nothin'. He go on grinnin' an' tole me the box holds air which you can't live but a few minutes without and that's what make it so valuable. I have to low he's right about that but I tole him if it got air in it it ain't empty an' that make me feel better.

Jeb Turner was real mad yesterday. He say he was over to Central City t'other day an' helt a door open for a lady an' she just look at him an' say, "I'd of done the same for you." He say she must be one of them liberty women you hear about an' what make him mad was he didn't think until he get home that he could of tole her he would of thank her.

Speakin' about gettin' mad I get mad at that smart aleck Craig Jamison. He say to me that Chickpea is a great town to be from an' the fromer you are the better. I wants to say I'd like to see him from it but I keep still 'cause Mr. Jamison is nice about givin' me credit.

They had a bad fire over at Stillwell's yesterday. When the volunteer fire truck gets there their brakes was so bad they went a mile past the fire before they could stop. By the time they gets turnt around an' drives back to the fire the house has done burnt to the ground.

Dink Porter's uncle give him a billy goat an' it smelt so bad Stew Borders ask Dink how long it been dead.

Miss Thornberry still can't get her mind off eddycation. Now she is sayin' Chickpea should have a library and what they need is a filanthrofist to give the money for it. I looks all through the f's in my dictionary to find out what a filanthrofist is and it ain't in the book so maybe I bought me a bad dictionary after all.

The ladies of the Chickpea Garden Club had some big city lady give them a talk on somethin' call ettyket and now they is all eatin' dinner instead of supper and burnin' candles on the table. If they ain't careful they is goin' to burn Chickpea down some night.

That Craig Jamison is gettin' on other folks' nerves. Bill Johnson is one of them an' he told me Craig ain't ever goin' to be like that Plato. Bill tole me one time there was a bad flood in Chickpea an' half the county was under water. He say he remark to Plato this is a lot of water an' Plato say, "An' you is only lookin' at the top of it."

That's all the news for now.

Cousin Hank

P.S. Somebody donate a pile of concrete blocks to that faker, Sister Kaye, who call herself a preacher so she can build herself a building and there was enough fool men been listenin' to her to put them together so they looks like a church. It make the decent people down at Caney Church real mad 'cause she ain't nothin' but a false profit.

5
Chickpea
U.S.A.

Dear Cousin Elrod:

I finally gets some real news to write you. Mr. Jamison, the hardware man, went an' hire himself a bookkeeper some months ago. Now it turn out she been keepin' more than the books and he had her arrested. Since it don't amount to more than twenty-five dollars, Stew Borders ask Mr. Jamison why he didn't just fire her. Jamison say he want to see justice done and Stew tole him if he want to see justice done don't look for it in the Court House. Anyway, the bookkeeper get a probation sentence. I always thought probation was when you die an' leaves a will, so I don't know if Mr. Jamison get his justice or not.

Dink's dad give him a bicycle for his birthday an' Dink is wild about it. Says it's like sittin' down an' walkin'. Last Christmas I asks Dink if he believes in Santa Claus and Dink say, "No. It's like the devil. It's your daddy."

Nobody is satisfied these days. With Christmas comin' most folks says they want a snow an' when they gets it they fusses about it. The weather reports say snow or maybe rain, clear or maybe cloudy. It's like them weathermen can't make up their minds neither. I guess that's why it's called weather—they don't know weather it'll rain or snow or what.

I drops in on Bill Johnson t'other day. He was eatin' some fish he told me was smelt. Now if I had some fish that smelt I sure wouldn't eat it.

I went to the Good Samaritan Hospital to see Pat Wilburn. His bull throwed him over a fence last evening. I tole him I was sorry he had such a accident, but he lowed it weren't no accident. His bull did it on purpose.

Mr. Winterbottom's father die and I went to the funeral parlor to pay my respecks. Winterbottom is one of them people who won't admit to anything goin' wrong. When I ask him what his father die of he say it weren't nothin' serious.

I was over at Central City with Stew Borders one day an' he helt a door open for a little old lady. A young man tole Stew he was chivalrous. Stew got real mad an' chase that feller clear to Main Street but couldn't catch him. When he came back he tole me if he could of caught that feller he'd have kilt him. When I tole Stew what chivalrous mean he feel real bad an' say if he could catch that feller he'd like to apologize but the feller run too fast.

Miss Pinwhistle's niece from Central City come over for a visit an' Mrs. Ambrose ask them over for tea an' sanwidges. Miss Pinwhistle's niece ask what kind of sanwidges they is an' when Mrs. Ambrose tell her they is finger sanwidges she throw up.

I been learnin' a lot readin' that dictionary I buy. I finds out t'other night what cornucopia mean. Here all these years I been thinkin' it is a foot disease.

I walk up to Rubin Flener yesterday—he's the village idiot, you remember, an I asks him what he is doin'. He says, "Thinkin'." An' I asks him what is he thinkin' about an' he says, "Nothin'."

That's all the news for now.

Cousin Hank

P.S. You remember I writ you about somebody givin' that faker, Sister Kaye, a passel of concrete blocks for a church building. Well, I find out it was Jerry Blumer who run the Lions Den Saloon. I think he give it as a thank offerin' for her drivin' all them digustit husbands to drink. I reckon he figger if it rain he won't lose no money 'cause she can preach indoors an' he hope the roof don't leak.

6

Chickpea
U.S.A.

Dear Cousin Elrod:

A lot of women from the big city comes to Chickpea lookin' for antiques. They buys a lot of furniture here from women whose husbands has made it and left it out in the rain for a few days. These wives tell the city women the furniture has been handed down in their families. The only handin' down this furniture ever see is when the husbands hands it to their wives. Some of these women says they is lookin' for period furniture and Mel Thurman, the guard down at the State Prison in Central City says send them to him. They got a piece of period furniture at the prison call the electric chair.

I don't know if you remember John Clancy or not. He's the railroad engineer who live in Chickpea. Well, he has a autymobile, but he don't drive it very often an' when he come to a curve it seem he is so use to bein' on a track he sometime forget to turn the steerin' wheel an' run off the road. Last week when he come to a railroad crossin' he blow his horn instead of stoppin' an' nearly get hit by old 33. He don't need insurance. When folks sees him comin' they gets out of his way.

I was talkin' to Mrs. Winterbottom yesterday about the govment puttin' a man in space and she low that NASA bunch ought to come to Chickpea. She say there is more space in the men's heads here than NASA will ever need.

They was a big fight down at the Cracker Barrel Gen. Store

t'other day. Them farmers was settin' around the stove an' spittin' tobacco juice an' tellin' how much tobacco they raises on a acre. Craig Carothers get to braggin' an' claim he raise twice as much as them other farmers when Stew Borders ask him how big a acre was he talkin' about. Stew is one of them fellers who'll say anything. One day a govment man was askin' him how much corn he was goin' to raise an' Stew tole him he don't know. The govment man look surprise and say, "You don't know?" Stew shot back, "I'll tell you how much I'm goin' to plant, but I don't know how much will grow." Stew always claim he stick up for his friends. One day someone say Bob Potts don't have the sense of a mule an' Stew say he did. One time Stew was a witness in court an' after he get swore in the judge ask him if he were goin' to tell the truth. I remembers Stew sayin', "Judge, I wouldn't tell a lie to hurt my worst enemy—but to help a friend. . . . "

Clint Stover graduate from High School at the head of his class an' his parents is real proud of him. They can't afford to send him to college an' he is now a clerk at the Cracker Barrel Gen. Store. What get me all rile up is that Jake Scoggins is goin' to college after graduatin' at the bottom of the class. I learn he's goin' on a basketball scholarship. When you says Clint everybody say, "He's a smart kid." But when you says Jake they gets real excited an' says, "Boy! Can he play basketball!" Brains don't seem to be worth much these days.

Last year when Coon Creek overflow it flood Jeb Stillwell's farm an' cover his pay lake which he had stock with all kinds of fish. All his fish swims off an' Jeb say it like to bankruptured him.

That's all the news for now.

Cousin Hank

7

Chickpea
U.S.A.

Dear Cousin Elrod:

As usual there ain't much happen in Chickpea since I last writ you. But Ezra Moore has just get back from a visit to your city of Chicago and he is all excited over eatin' in some restaurant he say is call a cafeteria. He tole us you slides your tray down something that look like railroad tracks in front of a whole lot of food which he say is behind glass so you can't reach in an' help yourself but has to let some ladies all dress in white like nurses put it on plates and hand it to you. He say his uncle who take him there say you can get a well-balance meal at this place. Stew Borders ask him what a well-balance meal is and Ezra say he guess it is one you gets to the table without spillin' nothin'. He also tole us you got a streetcar in Chicago what go under the ground which don't bother him so much 'cause he is on a train once what go in a hole in a mountain. But he say it kind of scairt him when the streetcar go up in the air, but he calm down when his uncle tole him it was suppose to do this.

That Stew Borders can't stan' it if somebody tell somethin'. He got to tell somethin' better or he can't sleep, so he up an' tell us he was almost arrested in a big city once when he eat at one of them fancy restaurants. He tole us he started to walk out without payin' when they stop him. He tole the manager the waitress give him a piece of paper which say guest check an' where he come from you don't ask your guest to pay for nothin'. He told us he argue with them until they say they have him lock up if he don't pay an' that convince him.

Caney Church and the Nazarene Tabernacle decides one day that Chickpea is too small a town to have two churches so they calls a meetin' to merge theyselfs into one church which everbody thinks is a great idea. But some fanatics gets to speakin' an' the meetin' bust up in a fight an' them fanatics walks out an' forms a church of their own an' now we got three churches in Chickpea. There just ain't enough religion in Chickpea for three churches so I start goin' to Mount Caramel Church in Central City.

There was a near riot when word went around that Doc Storkbill shot Miss Pinwhistle for talkin' too much. But everbody feel real foolish when they find out what really happen was he give her a shot for lockjaw after she step on a rusty nail. I don't think such a rumer would of start if it had been anybody but that blabbermouth, Miss Pinwhistle.

After that writer feller give a talk to the Ladies Auxiliary over to Miss Cranbock's restaurant Mrs. Shotwell is goin' around town tellin' everbody her husband is a writer, too. He writes insurance.

Somebody said Miss Thornberry, the retire school teacher, has a Thesaurus. But Stew Borders say that can't be 'cause them dinasewers has been dead for years.

That's all the news for now.

Cousin Hank

8

Chickpea
U.S.A.

Dear Cousin Elrod:

Caney Church done get rid of their old organ an' buy a new one. Stew Borders, one of the Deacons, is goin' around tellin' everbody Caney Church had a organ transplant.

Luke Porter an' I was talkin' to Koko, the ninety-five year old Indian what live on the outskirts of Chickpea an' Luke was pointin' out the asphalt streets an' the houses an' other evidences of civilization to Koko an' sayin' ain't it wonderful what man an' the Lord had done to the country. Koko, he get a far away look in his eye an' say, "You should of seen it when the Lord had it by Himself."

Ever since Jim Smith who run the billiard parlor inherit all that money from his uncle he been spellin' his last name with a y an' addin' a e on it. He say this is the way his ancestors spelt it but I think it's 'cause he get the big head, or maybe his ancestors didn't know how to spell.

Luke Porter's little boy, Dink, eat supper with the Stillwell's t'other night. When he come back home he tole his folks the food was so bad it almos' make him sick. He say the Stillwells even thanks God for it. He go on to say that if the Stillwell's had eat first they wouldn't have give thanks.

I see the Post Office is shortenin' the breviations of States names. I hears this is one of them things they does to save money. If they saves any money the politicians will take it an' give themselves a raise. Stew Borders say if you have to have a license to run a automobile them politicians should have to have a license to run the govment.

I was over to one of them Supermarkets in Central City an' see them sellin' artificial eggs. Next thing they'll be sellin' artificial chickens. They was so many people in that place they like to crush me to death. No wonder they calls that place a Maul.

You remember Mr. Estes? He's the man who own one of them Cyclopedic Brittentanicas which he is always quotin' out of. T'other day Glave Robards get tired of listenin' to him an' say, "If you so smart, why ain't you rich?" Estes just smile an' tap his head an' say, "I'm rich up here." He know Glave ain't got no money neither.

Mr. Estes is ball headed an' he ain't speakin' to Stew Borders since Stew ask him if he got his scalp on upside down.

T'other day the fellers at the Cracker Barrel Gen. Store gets to arguin' if you eats soup or drinks it. If they puts as much effort on their farms as they does on those dumb arguments they could all retire early.

Dink Porter's eighth birthday is comin' up an' I suggests we buys him a book, but Stew Borders say get him something else 'cause he got a book. We gets to talkin' about thinkin' down at the Cracker Barrel Gen. Store an' Mr. Estes who use to be a school teacher say it have something to do with electricity in the brain. I guess that's why there ain't much thinkin' goin' on in Chickpea. Most of us has dead batteries. That's all the news for now.

Cousin Hank

P.S. Bill Johnson's brother Joe is got all kinds of trouble since he get old but he brag he is still on his feet. I don't tell him but I think his feet is on his last legs.

9

Chickpea
U.S.A.

Dear Cousin Elrod:

The population of Chickpea is still goin' backwards. That beer-drinkin' Blackton boy who run the garage here in Chickpea was workin' under a truck loaded with beer t'other day when the jack slip an' he gets kilt. This don't surprise nobody 'cause we all been sayin' beer was goin' to kill him someday.

Miss Pinwhistle, who everbody call a busy-body, went in the Good Samaritan Hospital for a gall bladder operation. Evan Walker say it might help 'cause she got too much gall already. I don't think it help any, 'cause Miss Spears who visit her come back and repeat some of the things Miss Pinwhistle say about the nurses and the interns at the hospital.

You remember the Porter's? Well their son, Jim, graduate from one of them big colleges and come back for a visit to Chickpea. He use to talk real nice but now he talk somethin' awful. He tole me that where he went the boys and girls matriculate together on the campus and even use the same curriculum. I'm glad he's openin' his accountin' office in New York. He also tole me he has got one degree and is goin' back for some more. I reckon he'll end up with more degrees than one of them centipede thermometers.

We had a unusual thing happen t'other day. Mangus Stump's

brother kilt himself. His wife, Minnie, say he set down an' start to worry an' then shoot himself. Ezra Moore say he guess he's real lucky 'cause when he sets down and worry he fall asleep. Ezra's wife say he is always fallin' asleep. I asks Ezra if he enjoys sleepin' an' he say he don't know, he is unconscious when he do it.

I writ you I bought one of them dictionary books which I thought would help me understand what I was readin' since what I was readin' don't make no sense when I don't know what all the words means an' it still don't make no sense when I does.

The Town Council finally hire a policeman. They gives the job to Alvin White since he's the only one in town who own a pistol. I thinks he is a good choice 'cause they wants him to work at night an' ever time I see him in the daytime he is asleep so he shouldn't have no trouble stayin' awake nights.

I don't know why we needs a policeman in Chickpea anyway. The only crime I ever hear of committed here was when Henry Ambrose's house was broke into by Danny Mings. The lawyers gets to arguin' whether it is burglary or housebreakin' which is base on how light or dark it is an' carry different punishments. They takes so long arguin' that Henry jump up an' say all he want is his shotgun back. Danny claims it's his shotgun which he loan Henry and Henry never give back. After they decide it was burglary they couldn't get witnesses to prove whose shotgun it is so Judge Turner settle it by asking Henry and Danny to forget whose gun it is an' give it to the Town Council of Chickpea so the policeman can use it in case of an emergency. Henry and Danny agrees but is sorry they does when they sees Judge Turner rabbit huntin' with it that fall.

A lot of folks around here goes to Koko, the Indian, to get treated for their ailments. He is what you calls a herb doctor an' some think he is better than Doc Storkbill but I thinks the real reason they goes to him is 'cause he don't charge as much an' never recommend one of them fancy operations that cost a lot of money.

Henry Estes who is a retire school teacher an' know a lot of things tole us down at the Cracker Barrel Gen. Store t'other day that they is some opry singers can hit a high note an' break a wine glass if it ain't settin' too far away. Stew Borders up an low he reckon Miss Thornberry who sing in the choir at Caney Church could hit one of her high notes an' break out a street light if she try hard enough.

Stew Borders who is one of them fellers who is always worryin' about himself tole me whenever he is takin' a trip he always try to eat in a hospital restaurant if he can 'cause if you get sick help is close at hand.

That's all the news for now.

Cousin Hank

10

Chickpea
U.S.A.

Dear Cousin Elrod:

You can't tell where a frog'll hop from where it's settin'. The minister of Caney Church run off with the organist and the congregation lets out a howl like a buzz saw goin' through a walnut log. Everbody think it is 'cause of what the minister do but it turn out that the lamentation is on account of the population go down by two. It look like Chickpea is tryin' to counterack the population explosion everbody is talkin' about.

I been readin' how them Japanese is buyin' up most of the United States. If we don't want them to take over we better hurry up an' make them a state.

Did I write you the latest about Koko the Indian? Well, he been sellin' jewelry he say he get from his relatives on the reservation an' he been doin' real well. But t'other day he forget to take off a Made in Japan label an' his business suffer considerable.

That Stew Borders is a smart aleck. I asks him what time it is an' he look at his watch an' say he can't tell 'cause his watch got its hands in front of its face. I gets even with him. I tole him his watch must be bashful an' this make him mad 'cause he don't like no one to go him one better.

I sees by that television contraption that everbody is worryin' about what they is eatin' these days. Heck, Elrod, I still ain't forget the depression when all we worry about was if we was goin' to eat or not. Today everbody is worryin' about collessterall and yesterday it was salt. You remember when we was little they tell us to stay out of the sun? An' then everbody started layin' out in the sun an' gettin' suntans and now they're back tellin' us to stay out of the sun 'cause it give you cancer. You just don't know what to do these days so I guess I'll just quit worryin' about it. I bet if you looks at all this commotion close enough you'll find it's cause by folks tryin' to sell you somethin'. I remember that feller Plato sayin' if you scratch anything you'll find money at the bottom of it.

Somebody has nickname Mordecai Collier's little boy "Comb" cause he's at that age where he get in everbody's hair. By the way, Mordecai bein' the banker is able to afford one of them garage doors you can open an' shut from your car by pointin' some kind of a gadjit at it which make a noise. Mordecai say it's this noise which do the trick. Well, since a lot of airyplanes fly over his house his garage doors has been goin' up an' down like Miss Pinwhistle's mouth an' it's near drove Mordecai crazy. This just go to show that the more money you has the more trouble you has.

I was down at West Bennet's Federal Building t'other day when Mrs. Smith, or Smythe, as they calls theyselves these days since they is rich, come in an' walk back to the room where West sell his postage stamps for the govment. She is totin' her four-year-old son, Darrell, on her hip an' he is bawlin' his lungs out. I asks her if he is sick an' she say, "No. He think I brung him down here to send him back where he come from."

Tobey Maddox who run the garage in Central City charge me twenty-dollars for doin' almost nothin' t'other day. My car was makin' a funny kind of knock an' after he listen to it for a short spell he taken a hammer an' tap on it an' the noise stop an' the car run right good again. I asks him how come he charge me twenty-dollars for just tappin' on my motor with a hammer an' a small one at that an' he say he charge me five cents for tappin' an' nineteen-dollars an' ninety-five cents for knowin' where to tap.

You remember how everbody you meet was proud of Chickpea an' was glad they live here? Well, we all likes to brag on our town but we is kind of ashamed of the town square which we don't talk about much 'cause it's so small you can spit tobacco juice across if it the wind ain't blowin'.

Troy Conners get in some kinda trouble with the law an somebody tole him he need to get him a criminal lawyer an' Troy low one oughtn't be hard to find 'cause most of them is criminals theyselfs.

That's all the news for now.

Cousin Hank

11

Chickpea
U.S.A.

Dear Cousin Elrod:

The only thing happen in Chickpea lately was they arrests Lum Keller again for sellin' moonshine. He get real mad an' he tole the judge the only difference between him an' Jerry Blumer who run the Lion's Den Saloon is Jerry got a license to break the law.

I don't think I tole you about the time I went to the Big City with Mr. Winterbottom an' he insist we eat in one of them fancy restaurants where you can't read the menu 'cause it is writ in French. Well, Winterbottom who always claim to know everthin' an' won't ever admit to makin' no mistake say he can handle them menus an' after we sets down he order somethin' call escargots. I just asks the waiter, who Winterbottom call Mr. Garson, to bring me some bake chicken. After Mr. Garson puts the meal on the table Winterbottom look at his plate an' get a real funny look on his face. But he go ahead an' eat ever bit of them escargots like he been doin' it ever day. While Mr. Garson is clearin' the plates off the table he ask Mr. Winterbottom how he like the escargots. Mr. Winterbottom he look Mr. Garson in the eye an' say, "If I weren't a old escargot eater, I would of swore them was snails."

I been lookin' for Koko to get arrested for selling somethin' he call a nostrum which is full of alcohol and which he say is good for any ailments like gout, artheritis, nervousness, and whatever it is you got includin' ballness. People who don't drink buys it all the time. I never see it cure no ballness but that is 'cause nobody will waste it by pourin' it on their head. Somebody ask me once what kind of a Indian Koko is an' I say he is either a Navaho or a Zucchini.

Stew Borders own a lot over in Central City an' somebody offer him the sum of one thousand dollars for it an' Stew say he don't want some of it, he want all of it.

Henry Estes was sayin' down at the Cracker Barrel Gen. Store t'other day how important electricity is and that without it we wouldn't have no electric lights, radio, or television. He even say he got a cousin with heart trouble who run on a contraption that has a battery just like a automobile. I wish that Plato feller who live here some years ago was still around. I'd like to know what he would say about all this. Incidently, everbody sets around the stove down at the Cracker Barrel Gen. Store tryin' to think of somethin' wise to say so people will call them Plato one day. I figger all they has to do is say somethin' you can't understand.

Word get to Stew Borders that the Radcliff family what just move to Chickpea has got a tow-headed boy an' that dumbbell like to of start a riot tellin' folks the Radcliff's had a two-headed boy. By the time they gets it straighten out they had done ruin the Radcliff's front yard.

Radcliffs is a large family an' we are glad they move here 'cause it get our population back to 1,199 an' this include Mrs. Bramliff's baby which didn't turn out to be twins like Miss Cranbock hope.

Another one of them speakers come to Chickpea to talk to the Ladies Auxiliary at Miss Cranbock's restaurant. I heared he tole them about a feller name Karl Marx. I would have like to hear that myself 'cause I didn't know there was a Marx brother name Karl.

I was talkin' to Miss Thornberry an' Miss Pinwhistle yesterday an' Miss Thornberry tole us she heared Jim Smith who run the billiard hall has a brother in Chicago who is a bookmaker an' Miss Pinwhistle up an low she'd like to meet him if he ever visit Chickpea 'cause she ain't never met no writers.

We was talkin' t'other day down at the Cracker Barrel Gen. Store about friends an' friendship an' how nice it was to have a close friend an' Stew Borders up an' say the closest friend he ever have was a feller who wouldn't buy somebody a ten cent candy bar if they was two for a nickel.

Last week a new couple move to Chickpea an' that finally get our population over 1,200 an' up to 1,201 according to the last count. Stew Borders tole me they come from a foreign country but they can speak our language real good. I ask him what country they is from an' he tell me they is from New Mexico.

That's all the news for now.

Cousin Hank

12

Chickpea
U.S.A.

Dear Cousin Elrod:

I don't have much to write you about 'cause Miss Pinwhistle an' Miss Thornberry has both been out of town for about a week, an' when they is gone it is like your radio is busted an' your newspaper not bein' on your front porch. But there was somethin' happen that is goin' to break their hearts when they gets back an' finds out they missed bein' able to tell everbody about it an' that is what Doc Storkbill do t'other night, or rather t'other morning. I tell you, Elrod, there just ain't nobody like old Doc Storkbill anywheres. It seem Steve Weller wake up about two o'clock in the morning an' yell somethin' awful accordin' to his wife, Nora, who tole me he was sufferin' a powerful lot from a pain in his right side an' was throwin' up fastern she could wipe up. They calls Doc Storkbill an' he gets out of bed an' rushes out to the Wellers an' say Steve has got a very acute appendix an' that it has got to come out or Steve will die. So Doc puts Steve on the kitchen table an' washes his own hands real good an' then gives Steve a anesthetic an' takes out this appendix while Steve is sleepin'. Doc sets up all night with Steve an' when he think Steve is out of danger he finally go home. Natcherly he don't get no rest on account of he got other patients with troubles. Now you an' I knows good an' well old Doc ain't goin' to get pay very much at all, if he gets that much, for what he do for Steve Weller. I asks you, where is you goin' to get service like that anywheres except in a small town like Chickpea? You ain't goin' to get it in them big cities where they specializes in gunshot wounds which we don't have much of except when some hunter has a accident or that dumbbell Stew Borders shoot himself in the foot which he is likely to do anytime. I remembers you writin' me about your good friend who wake up one night feelin' poorly an' his wife take him to one of them big hospitals you got where instead of a doctor lookin' at him right away some lady say he has to answer a lot of questions first, especially 'bout how he is goin' to pay for what they will do for him an' while she is askin' him all these questions he die. An' then the hospital send his wife a bill. Another nice thing about Chickpea is you don't have to pay somebody for dyin'. I'm tellin' you, Elrod, you better think about comin' back here when you retires, especially if you ain't feelin' well.

I ain't aimin' to write you no book on medical history but I wants to tell you what happen to Travis Wilson an' them medical people. Travis tole me what he like about goin' to Doc Storkbill is 'cause Doc always fix you up himself an' he say he sure miss Doc when he get sick in one of them big cities once.

He say he went to a doctor who send him to some specialist who look him over an' send for somebody he call a insultant an' then these two Docs send him to another specialist who taken a lot of funny lookin' pictures of his insides. After all this commotion he say they tell him thay can't find nothin' wrong with him except he is run down a bit. They tells him to go home an' get some rest an' then come back in about two months. Travis say he settle for goin' home to get the rest 'cause he thought they was goin' to tell him to go home an' get some more money. He tole me he ain't goin' back 'cause Doc Storkbill fix him up real good with some vitamin pills.

I run into Stew Borders yesterday an' he was all excited. He tole me we is livin' in a marvelous age. He say one of his neighbors has got a contraption call a incubator which he connect to his electricity an' put a lot of eggs in it an' in three weeks it was full of chickens. Stew low it is marvelous what science is doin' an' now we can get chickens by machinery. He say he think it is sad them chickens not havin' parents an' that if he eat one he would feel like he was eatin' a orphan.

Tink Collins just come back from visitin' relatives in the big city an' he low he seen a woman who makes statues an' things out of mud an' bake them for a while. He says she make a lot of money sellin' little things she make this way an' say she make more money out of a bushel of dirt than all the farmers around Chickpea makes on acres of it. He say he seen a little figger of a man he know didn't take more than a handful of this mud to make an' she get over one-hunerd dollars for it. Stew Borders say it break his heart to hear this 'cause he couldn't raise a stalk of corn on that little mud.

That's all the news for now.

Cousin Hank

13

Chickpea
U.S.A.

Dear Cousin Elrod:

Talk is all over town about Mordecai Collier buyin' a furnace from one of them salesmen from the city. After he get it put in his house Mordecai find out it's a gas furnace an' Chickpea don't have no gas lines so he feel quite bad. But Glave Robards fix it up for him so he can use bottle gas an' this make him feel better. But his wife tell everbody this just goes to show he's as dumb as she always say he is.

Mr. Jamison tole the fellers down at the Cracker Barrel Gen. Store that if his father was livin' today he would be one-hunerd-three years old. Stew Borders say his father die twenty-five years ago an' if he were still livin' he'd be miserble.

Stew Borders ask me to go with him again to Doc Storkbill's. Stew is always imaginin' there is somethin' wrong with him an' Miss Thornberry who know a long word for just about anything say he is a hippocrontrack or somethin'. While we is at Doc's one of his patients walks out an' drops dead in front of his office. Doc get all excited an' say, "What can I do?" an' Stew say, "Turn him aroun' so it look like he was comin' in."

Whenever Stew go over to Doc Storkbill Doc check him over an' always prescribe the same little white pill which fix Stew up real good until he get it in his head he has got somethin' else wrong with him. Miss Thornberry tole me she think Doc Storkbill give Stew a placebo. That placebo pill must be real good medicine for it sure do make Stew feel good for a while.

Dink Porter, that little eight-year-old, is always askin' questions an' t'other day when he was in the Cracker Barrel Gen. Store with his ma he ask what a second language was. None of them fellers what sit around the stove could make him understan' although they tries real hard. Finally Jim Smith tole him it was like if a dog learnt how to say meow. Dink's face lit up an' he say, "Oh, I see." So I guesses he do at that an' Jim ack like he was real proud of himself.

Pat Wilburn tole me he goes over to Doc Storkbill to see if Doc can do any more for his artheritis and Doc tole him to exercise an' Pat say he remind him that he tole him last month not to exercise. Pat say Doc hesitate a moment an' then say, "Ain't it remarkable what progress medicine has made in a month!"

That Stew Borders has got a answer for everthin'. They was talkin' down at the Lion's Den Saloon about what you call a person who don't believe in birth control an' Stew say, "A parent."

Millard Shotwell tole Jim Smith his son, Abraham, who study law, pass his examination for a license an' was admitted to the bar in Kentucky. Jim say it's hard for him to believe a state what make as much whisky as Kentucky would make you take a test an' give you a license to go in a bar. He say in Chickpea you only needs a license to sell whisky not to drink it.

Doc Storkbill tole Miss Pinwhistle the major cause of headaches in women was housework, but Troy Conner's wife, Mabel, say it's husbands.

I was walkin' on Main Street with Mr. Winterbottom when we runs into John Clancy, the railroad engineer I may have writ you about. Well, this Clancy was lookin' like a statue of hope gone an' I asks him, "What is the matter?"

An' he tole us he has just read a railroad magazine what say the railroad he work for has the shortest mileage of track of all railroads in the country an' it make him sad. You know Winterbottom, who have a way of justifyin' everthing he say or do, well he cheer Clancy up when he tell him, "Them other companies might have longer tracks than yours but they ain't no wider."

Everbody in Chickpea is glad to see spring get here except West Bennet. He say most folks in Chickpea raises a garden an' it hurts his business down at the Cracker Barrel Gen. Store. Stew Borders say he don't feel too sorry for him 'cause there is enough people livin' in Chickpea too lazy to raise a garden to make any difference.

I say to Stew Border t'other day that Rubin Flener, the village idiot, seem to have such a easy mind an' Stew says this is 'cause he has such a poor memory.

That's all the news for now.

Cousin Hank

14

Chickpea
U.S.A.

Dear Cousin Elrod:

We was all over at a play given at the High School in Central City t'other night. It was a play call Othello an' was writ by some feller who live in England a long time ago by the name of William Shakespere. They come to a part in this play where this Othello feller is tryin' to get his wife whose name is Desdemonia to give him a handkerchief an' she won't do it. Othello keep on askin' her over an' over an' finally Stew Borders who is settin' in the front row yells out to him, "Use your coat sleeve an' get on with the play." Everbody from Chickpea was awful embarrass.

Rubin Flener tell me he won't stan' up if he can set down or set down if he can lay down. I don't know if he's lazy or smart when he talk like this. T'other day Mr. Jamison see him standin' in front of his store an' he run him off an' Rubin tole him to go jump in the lake. When Rubin's mother hear about this she make Rubin go back an' apologize. So Rubin go up to Mr. Jamison an' say, "You don't have to jump in the lake. My mother an' I has made other arrangements."

Mangus Stump an' his wife, Wilma, is havin' a awful time with young Myron. They got him so spoilt all he do is cry an' throw tantums to get his way an' they can't do nothin' with him. Somebody tole them Doc Storkbill study sycology, whatever that is, once an' say they should take Myron over an' let

Doc treat him with some of this sycology stuff. I happens to be in the office when they comes in with Myron who is whoopin' an' hollerin' an' carryin' on somethin' awful. After they explains the situation to Doc he walk over to Myron an' whisper somethin' in his ear an' Myron calm down an' start actin' real nice. After the Stumps leave I asks Doc what kind of sycology did he use on Myron that work so well an' Doc say, "I tell him if he don't shut up an' behave himself I was gonna womp the tar outen him."

West Bennet nearly get himself in trouble. The City Council hear he got a sign in his store sayin' candy bars ten cents, two for a quarter. They sends Alvin White around to talk to him an' tell him he will get lock up if he try to cheat the public like this. Alvin quotes some truth or consequences law. West Bennet say he just tryin' to have a little fun but I see him take the sign down in a hurry anyway.

Them educators over at Central City done lose their minds. They got a three day course in automobile drivin' which they call a crash course. Them teenagers don't need no lessons on how to have a accident.

Walt Blanton was complainin' to me t'other day that he is goin' ball. I tole him I heared that Plato feller had say be glad hair ain't like teeth an' hurt an' has to be pull out.

Luke Porter tole me t'other day he send his little boy, Dink, to the performacy to get some pills an' the druggist feller ask him if he want him to put them in a box. Luke like to die laughin' when he tole me Dink ask that performacist, "What do you expec' me to do? Roll them home?"

Stew Borders is always complainin' an' fussin' about somethin' an' now he is hollerin' about this daylight savin' thing. He say he wish them people what run the time would leave the sun alone 'cause he never was able to set his cows an' chickens back an' forth like he done his clock. He say this daylight savin' time make him get to Central City too late in the day an' he miss a lot of good movies on account of it in the summertime when he is farmin'. Miss Pinwhistle who taken a airyplane trip out of the country some years ago an' don't want people to forget it has been sayin' ever since that turnin' her clock forward in the springtime give her somethin' she call jet lag. Personally I don't think it do. I think this is just her way of still braggin' after she done wore everbody out with the details.

Mr. Winterbottom who won't admit to no criticism was settin' down at the Cracker Barrel Gen. Store with us t'other day an' say somethin' about never bein' sick an' he knock on wood when he say it. I asks him if he is superstitious an' he say, "No. I ain't supersititious. I just don't take no chances."

That's all the news for now.

Cousin Hank

15

Chickpea
U.S.A.

Dear Cousin Elrod:

I tole Stew Borders the nice thing about livin' in a small town is you gets to know everthin' about everbody. But he say the drawback is they gets to know everthin' about you, too. He is always takin' the pleasure out of life.

I'm glad, Elrod, that I was borned and growed up an' stay in Chickpea. Did you ever notice how them small town boys who works hard an' saves so they can go to the big city works hard an' saves when they gets there so they can retire an' come back to a small town an' enjoy life? I never heared of a big city feller workin' all his life in a small town so he could retire an' live in a big city.

They finally gets a new pastor for Caney Church. It is a feller name of Matthew Tatum who was a farmer till he get the call to preach. Personally, I think farmin' get too much for him to handle as he get older on account of he is always sayin' if you don't behave yourself God will send you to a place where the punishment is worser than plowin' on a day in July.

Jason Gump's dog, Tyron, die t'other day an' Jason ask Rev. Tatum if he'll bury Tyron. Tatum say he don't bury no dogs 'cause they ain't got no soul an' Jason say he is right disappointed an' that he was goin' to pay a hunerd dollars to get Tyron buried an' Rev. Tatum say, "Why didn't you tell me Tyron was a Christian?"

I meets Miss Thornberry on Main Street yesterday an' she look powerful sad.

I asks her what is the matter an' she tole me the more she talk to her former pupils the sadder she get. She low she did a heap of teachin' but they didn't do much learnin'.

Miss Pinwhistle say the only thing she don't like about livin' in a small town is everbody know your age. There's always somebody around who remembers when you was born an' nine time out of ten it's the town gossip, she say.

You can always tell when West Bennet has been to one of them business conventions in the big city where he hobnob with them important executive fellers an' company presidents. For two weeks he go around callin' everbody by their initials. He like to drive us crazy with his "Hello, J.B.," "How are you H.A. an' M.T.?" Miss Thornberry say he is sufferin' from a temperary superiority complexion. Fortunately for everbody in Chickpea he always get over it.

He get to sufferin' from another of them complexions t'other day. He get the first wanted poster from the govment to put on the wall of the room he sell his stamps in. He was so excited we thought he was goin' to frame it afore he hung it up.

I think I writ you before that Stew Borders is just about the dumbest person I ever know. If Rubin Flener ever die Stew could replace him as the village idiot. T'other day one of them city women was in town lookin' for antiques an' she ask Stew's wife, Becky, if there was a Ante Bellum house in Chickpea. Stew was standin' there an' he up an' tell her there ain't nobody's auntie by that name livin' in Chickpea.

Some smart aleck city feller stop his car an' ask me directions t'other day 'cause he say he is lost an' is tryin' to get to Central City. After I gives him his directions he ask me the name of this town he is in an' when I tole him it is Chickpea he laugh an' say, "What do you citizens call yourselfs—Garbanzans?" This make me so mad I tell him I am not lost an' that he must be powerful dumb to get himself lost in a place as small as Chickpea.

I just remembers somethin' before I closes an' that is that Winterbottom feller who is always tryin' to be so percise about things tole us the Kentucky Derby ain't a horse race. When we tell him it is he look real wise an' say it is run by three year old thoroughbreds what is call colts an' this make it a colt race. I likes what Arnold Dinglehoffer tole him. He tole Winterbottom if he call it a colt race in Looyville they would run him plumb out of Kentucky.

That's all the news for now.

Cousin Hank

16

Chickpea
U.S.A.

Dear Cousin Elrod:

That Indian I mention to you before by the name of Koko also does some docterin' of animals and sometimes of people, especially if they is too poor to go to Doc Storkbill although Doc will treat them for free if they can't pay which is why he is a poor folk himself. Anyways, Estil Courtney's wife Vera who'll do most anything to get out of payin' goes to Koko for his free treatment. But when she get the mange in her hair she goes to Doc Storkbill sayin' she ain't lettin' no Indian get his hands on her scalp.

Doc Storkbill gets him a assistant doctor right out of medical school an' he think he is goin' to be able to take it easy, but the younggun quits after two months when people begins payin' him with stuff out of their gardens. When Jethro Crump pay him with a bushel of pole beans he say he want cash, but everbody know that's what Doc Storkbill charge for treatin' artheritis. They don't teach them new students nothin' practical no more.

Chickpea nearly get two new citizens. Mangus Stump tole

me his cousin Bill Hodges an' his wife Martha was gettin' ready to settle here but decides not to at the last minute. Bill tole Mangus he wanted to put his money in four banks so folks wouldn't know what he got but Mangus tole him that weren't possible 'cause Chickpea only got one bank. So Bill look around till he find a town with four banks an' move there. At least that's what Mangus tole me.

Doc Storkbill tole me Luke Porter, the real estate man, been comin' over to his office ever week for a checkup. Seems like he find a medical book left in a vacant house an' taken it home an' been gettin' ever disease he read about. Doc tole me them medical books sends him more patients than a flu epidemic.

Somebody ask Stew Borders if Doc ever treat his wife an' Stew say, "No, we have to pay him ever time."

Bill Johnson ask me what a nounce is an' I say I never heared of a nounce. After I spends three days goin' through my dictionary book an' can't find it I asks him where he heared of such a word an' he say Miss Thornberry tole him a nounce of pervention is worth a pound of cure.

Arnold Dinglehoffer has got one of them hound dogs that walks half sideways. Arnold say Bowser is a good huntin' dog but he can't get him to fetch him his slippers 'cause Bowser won't bring him nothin' unless he shoot it an' he ain't about to blow a hole in his ceiling to satisfy no dog.

You remember Hontas Stark, the town giant, who's over eight feet tall an' weigh three-hunerd pounds? Nobody'll play poker with him 'cause he got a pair of fists that'll beat a full house. Stew Borders say the only thing in Chickpea that's stronger than Hontas is the coffee down at Miss Cranbock's Diner.

Jethro Crump sure been fussin' a lot since them women in the Ladies Auxiliary has been gettin' ettyket which all start some time ago when some lady from the city give a talk on how to ack nice. Jethro says his wife is servin' salats at night an' puttin two forks on the table. He tole us he ask his wife what she is doin' puttin' two forks on the table all of a sudden an' she tole him one is a salat fork an' is just for eatin' your salat. He

says them salats is usually raw green stuff an' he feel like he is
bein' put out to pasture every time he eat one. Henry Ambrose
up an' say him an' his wife was visitin' some friends in the big
city once an' after they eat their supper these folks puts a little
cup an' saucer in front of him an' tells him it is a demi tass. The
little cup has got coffee in it, he tole us, an' when you drink it
you has to be careful you don't swallow the cup.

We was talkin' about old Doc Storkbill down at the Cracker
Barrel Gen. Store an' somebody remark he never heard of Doc
deliverin' twins. Stew Borders up an low that's 'cause Doc is
such a cheapskate he won't deliver two for the price of one.

That's all the news for now.

Cousin Hank

17
Chickpea
U.S.A.

Dear Cousin Elrod:

We had some real excitement in Chickpea yesterday. Mangus Stump went runnin' down the street yellin' a space ship
from Mars has just land on Kelly Vance's farm. Half of Chickpea run down there to see it an' two old ladies got trample in
the rush an' had to be taken to Doc Storkbill for treatment. The
other half of the town lock themselves in their houses with
shotguns on their laps. Doc Storkbill was mad 'cause he miss all
the excitement tendin' to them two old ladies. But everthin'
calm down all at once when the space ship turn out to be one
of them hot air balloons.

Doc Storkbill has a ideal office for a small town. When you
sets in the waitin' room you can hear everthin' that go on when
he is tendin' to his patients. T'other day I was settin' there when
one of them town gossips is gettin' examine an' I heared Doc
tell her she need plenty of rest an' she say, "How can you tell
me that? All you has me do is stick out my tongue." An' Doc
say, "That's what need the rest."

Stew Borders get back from the dentist at Central City an' was he ever mad over what the dentist charge him! He say that dentist must think he invent the toothache.

Millard Stockwell's son, Abraham, was home from college on a vacation an' tole me he is majorin' in English but from the way he talk I think he is majorin' in basketball.

The citizens of nearby Central City is got right uppity since their city has got two one-way streets. I guess one is for comin' an' t'other is for goin'.

I was over at the dentist myself not long ago an' has to set there an' listen to a lot of singin' comin' outen a radio he have in his ceiling. I finally figgers he have this music goin' so if folks hears his patients screamin' they'll think it's the singin'.

Jethro Crump get on my nerves braggin' to me about the computer he get to help him run his bankin' business. It's a great big contraption an' got a room all to itself. I tole him I got a computer I carry around in my pocket that can do everthin' his computer can do an' I shows him my ball point pen.

They was talkin' t'other day down at the Cracker Barrel Gen. Store of when rural eletrocution brought electricity to Chickpea. People is so proud they burns their lights in the daytime as well as at night. But after they gets their first bill some don't even burn them at night. I was in Larry Jamison's hardware store t'other day to get out of the rain when one of them smart alecky city fellers come in an' ask Larry if he got anythin' to stop the rain. Larry keep a straight face an' say, "I just sell the last one."

Stew Borders an' me met Doc Storkbill at his son's funeral parlor where they was gettin' ready to bury one of Doc's patients an' Stew ask Doc if he was ever afeared of gettin' charge with premedicated murder.

We was talkin' down at the Cracker Barrel Gen. Store t'other day about finances an' Travis Wilson say we would all be better off if there weren't no such thing as money. Stew Borders up an' low if there weren't no such thing as money he couldn't be able to tell the difference.

We had us a awful scandal in Chickpea this year. It seem

Steve Weller's wife, Nora, who been winnin' a lot of blue ribbons at the county fair with her vegetables get caught cheatin'. This year she forget to take some kind of a label off one of the vegetables she claim to have raise in her garden an' one of the judges spy it. You read about stuff like this all the time in the newspapers about govment men an' such doin' all kinds of things they hadn't ought to but when it happen to somebody in your home town it make you feel real bad. One oldtimer say he remember that Plato feller what live here a long time ago sayin' when there is evil at the top it dribble down to everbody an' I reckon he is quite right at that.

Miss Pinwhistle get all upset. She heared somebody calls her a gossip. She say if folks in Chickpea hears somethin' they calls it gossip, but if they tells it they calls it news.

That's all the news for now.

Cousin Hank

18

Chickpea
U.S.A.

Dear Cousin Elrod:

Thank you for your last letter tellin' me what been goin' on in Chicago. Chicago seem like it is a lot like Chickpea only louder an' got more of everthing except peace an' quiet. I tell you, Elrod, I enjoy my visit with you last year except there wasn't much to do. Outside of you I don't have nobody to talk to an' there weren't no places to go to like the Cracker Barrel Gen. Store. Everthin' was just too much for me an' at night with all them lights you can't even see the stars. I think them people in Chicago is missin' a heap of fun. Who want to go out to all them places you got to be entertained? In Chickpea you can get all the entertainment you want walkin' down Main Street or listenin' to Miss Pinwhistle when she get wound up an' all this not costin' you a cent. I gets so tired smellin' all them autymobiles I would have give one of my Social Security checks just to smell a skunk. Besides, that big lake you got on the edge of town scare me. If it ever overflow it'll drown everbody.

You know, Elrod, I can't understand those men who sets around the stove at the Cracker Barrel Gen. Store. When they ain't chewin' tobacco they is smokin' an' I tell you they smokes up a storm. All you hears about these days from people who don't smoke is how dangerous this smokin' is. The only good I see comin' out of these fellers' smokin' is that when they are puffin' on them cigarets they can't talk a lot an' that give your ears a rest. One day when the smoke was real thick some stranger walk in an' when he see all this smoke he say, "Don't any of you inhale?" One of the fellers besides me who sets there an' don't smoke is Estil Courtney an' the reason he don't smoke is he can't afford to buy cigarets so he just set there an' take a lot of deep breaths an' I reckon he save a lot of money this way. Some wiseacre feller told West Bennet he better keep his windows close 'cause if people was to see the smoke comin' out somebody might call the fire department. I asks West once if all this smokin' don't hurt his business none by keepin' a lot of customers away an' West tell me he sell enough to the fellers around the stove to make up for it. If he sell them what they smoke he come out ahead. Arnold Dinglehoffer don't smoke an' he is always complainin' about it an' say he could smoke his hams at the Cracker Barrel Gen. Store. Danny Mings who believe everthing he hear say it wouldn't do no good 'cause them hams would taste terrible.

I tell you, Elrod, that Stew Borders friend of mine I write you about ever now an' then must be plumb outen his mind. Yesterday he start a near riot when he run out of his house an' yell, "They is a big snake down on the highway!" It was a nice day an' a lot of folks was out in their yards, I heared that them that wasn't listenin' to their television contraptions runs in the house an' locks theyselfs in. Them what was listenin' bust out laughin'.

It seem the man on the news had report that the electric men had a pylon on the highway an' that dumbbell Stew think he say a python which is one of them big snakes like a boa construction.

Mangus Stump has got a relative who growed up in the city an' never was in the country. Well, he come for a visit an' plan to spend some time with Mangus an' say he hope to get a good night's rest like he heared people in the country get. Well, at breakfast the day after he get here Mangus ask him how he sleep an' this relative tell Mangus he hardly sleep nary a bit what with all them barkin' dogs an' the brayin' of somebody's donkey an' some mockybird which start out singin' about midnight an' then them birds in the mornin' an' some old rooster soundin' off as soon as it get daylight. He say that night's sleep plumb wore him out. Then he ask Mangus what that hootin' sound was he heared now an' then an' Mangus tell him they never was able to figger out what it was but it come from the cemetery an' that was when this relative remembers some urgent business he have an' return home in a hurry. I guess some folks would rather smell them autymobiles. That Mangus has a lot of relatives livin' in the big city an' I remember one time when another relative come to see him an' tole Mangus he was walkin' on Main Street an' a couple of strangers speaks to him an' says "Hello." He say he say hello right back but keep on walkin' 'cause he is suspicious of strangers what speak to him. Mangus tole him that is the way folks is in a small town—real friendly-like an' everbody speak to everbody whether they knows them or not. This relative tole Mangus that if he speak to everbody he met in the big city he would have a sore throat before he even walk a block. When Mr. Winterbottom hear this he say he was in the big city once an' it was full of nothin' but strangers. He low he pray to see just anybody he knowed there even if it be his worse enemy.

That's all the news for now.

Cousin Hank

19

Chickpea
U.S.A.

Dear Cousin Elrod:

Do you remember me writin' you about the Stillwell house burnin' to the ground an' them losin' everthin'? Well, it seem Mr. Stillwell is right smart but not quite all the way right smart 'cause he have insurance which cover almost everthin' they has but he miss it by $1,000.00 an' they comes up that much short. But you knows how folks is in a small town. They looks out for each other an' the congregation down at Caney Church talks things over an' decides to take up a special collection an' raise the money the Stillwells lack an' give it to them.

Mordecai Collier almost throw a monkey wrench in things when he up an' say he know the Stillwells real good an' they is too proud to accept money like it is charity an' he propose they tells the Stillwells to pray to the Lord for the $1,000.00 so when the church give it to them they will think it come from the Lord. This is put up to the Stillwells who think it is a great idea an' then the congregation go about collectin' the money real quiet like so the Stillwells won't catch on. Well, they tries mighty hard but the best they can come up with is $500.00. After they sees this is all they can raise Rev. Tatum say, "Let's go ahead an' give them the $500.00 an' let it go at that." After everbody agree to this the Rev. Tatum call the Stillwells up to the front of the church the next Sunday an' present them with the $500.00 real proud like. Then he suggest to the Stillwells they says a prayer of thanks to the Lord for answerin' their prayer an' the Stillwells does this. I meets Mr. Stillwell on the street the next day an' he tole me he ain't never goin' to do somethin' like this again. He tole me after he get home an' count the money he say another prayer tellin' the Lord if he ever pray for money again to send it direct on account of the church took out half of it for itself.

The Town Council taken a pole on puttin' up a horseshoe court in the town square an' everbody was for it except West Bennet who was afeared the men would quit settin' around his stove in the Cracker Barrel Gen. Store which they does out of habit in the summertime when there ain't no need to keep warm an' this just goes to show how money influence a person. The Town Council appoint a committee to oversee this horseshoe court an' the first thing they finds out is that the town square ain't big enough. But the problem is resolve when Henry Ambrose say they can put in on a vacant lot he own next to his barber shop. Everbody think this is real nice of him but he does it 'cause he think it will help his business which has fell off somewhat since ever young man in Chickpea is lettin' his hair grow these days an' this is another example of what I say about money influencin' folks.

Word has been goin' around the Chickpea grapevine that when Miss Pinwhistle was in the big city visitin' some friends they taken her to a place name of White City which is one of them musement parks like you sees advertise on TV. It seem Miss Pinwhistle never been in one of them places before an' she come on some mirrors what makes folks look somethin' awful. The one she look in make her look real fat an' she get such a shock she pass out cold an' the park fellers has to send for a ambulance to revive her.

Once in a while in the wintertime Koko the Indian go what he say is deer huntin' an' you will see a skinned carcass hanging from a tree limb back of his house. Since there ain't many deer around these parts ever farmer nearby run out an' count his cows. I taken a good look at one of them carcasses once an' I think they better count their horses as well.

Did I ever tell you the first time Koko went in Jerry Blumer's Lion's Den Saloon to buy some whisky Jerry tole him he heared there was a law against sellin' firewater to Indians an' this make Koko so mad I think he is goin' on the warpath. But he find out he got enough friends to buy him all the firewater he need as long as he got the money to pay for it. Ever time Koko get drunk he put on a big feather thing that reach down to the ground an' start dancin' an' whoopin' an' hollerin' just somethin' awful. Sometime he get out a tommyhawk an' when he wave this around folks start runnin' for cover. We finally find out if we let him alone he'll take one drink too many an' pass out an' when he wake up he is always too sick to be dangerous, which I don't think he ever was in the first place. Folks is got use to him now an' don't pay him no attention when he get like this although his singin' and whoopin' do keep some folks awake.

That's all the news for now.

Cousin Hank

20

Chickpea
U.S.A.

Dear Cousin Elrod:

You remember that fake preacher name of Sister Kaye I writ you about? Well, when she first come to Chickpea she did some housecleanin' while she was gettin' her preachin' business started. I asks her to clean my house one day an' she tole me how some of them bachelor fellers in Chickpea keeps their houses an' say it is somethin' awful. She tole me Pat Wilburn have so much dirt on his floors she tole him he didn't need no rug, he could raise a cover crop instead. I bet Miss Pinwhistle would like to of talk to Sister Kaye!

I see these young fellers that is lettin' their hair grow real long is now gone to raisin' beards. I reckon this is so you can tell them from girls. Henry Ambrose who run the barber shop tole me this long hair business has just about bankruptered him.

Everbody is mad since the U.S. census figgers come out. You remember me writin' you how everbody been wantin' Chickpea to get its population over 1,200? Well, it seem the population done been over 1,200 for some time but nobody know it. Some folks gets curious an' they looks into it an' discovers those

idiots what calls theyselfs the Town Council an' been in charge
of countin' folks done forgets to count theyselfs. They is ten
people what ain't goin' to be in office next time Chickpea
choose a council.

One of them carnivals what has all kinds of rides an' games
an' I don't know what to get your money away from you come
to town last week an' stay for a few days. I always low they
stays as long as they feels safe an' gets out before they gets run
out. Well, anyway, Elrod, young Bill Staples go aroun' tellin'
folks his mother asks the fortune teller down at this carnival if
she can help her find the three-hunerd dollars she lose out of
her apron pocket. Bill tole everbody this fortune teller stare in
a object which look like a glass basketball an' tole Mrs. Staples
to look under a loose step in her cellar stairs. Bill say his mother
recall goin' in the cellar for some can goods an' when she look
under this broken step she find her three-hunerd dollars right
where it done fell out of her pocket. Of course this make
everbody run down to that fortune teller an' spend a lot of
money with her. After the carnival leave Bill Staples go aroun'
laughin' an' tellin' everbody the head carnival man pay him five
dollars for tellin' that story. Mr. Winterbottom who low
nobody ever fool him say he didn't believe the story 'cause he
knowed the Staples never has three-hunerd dollars in the first
place.

They got a bearded lady at this carnival but Stew Borders
say he don't believe it. He low it is a lady what wear a wig on
her face durin' workin' hours. Stew also tole me he heared they
has barkers at this carnival what stand outside tents an' tries to
get you to buy a ticket to go in an' see some kind of a exhibit.
Stew say he stand there an' listen to them for a long time but
never did hear one of them bark.

I was at this carnival one night with Stew Borders an' we sees
a tent with a sign on it what say Magician an' Stew say, "Let's
go in an' hear some music." I tell him he is mix up an' that a
magician is a man who make things disappear an' Stew say he
wish he'd brought his wife with him. Anyway, Stew puts a five
dollar bill down on a platform in front of this tent an' tole the

barker feller he want a ticket an' the barker feller say, "Go in." Stew ask him where is his change an' the feller tole Stew he give him the right amount of money. So Stew start to leave an' I asks him, "Ain't you goin' in to see the magician?" An' Stew say, "Ain't this the magician? He just make my money disappear."

Miss Pinwhistle say she went to the carnival an' the sideshow an' they give her the creeps. Stew low when he went there they didn't give him nothin'. He had to pay for everthin'.

Mrs. Flener taken her son Rubin, the village idiot, to the carnival an' Stew Borders advise her not to take him in the sideshow to see the freaks 'cause it might make him sad. Stew tole me later the real reason he say this is 'cause he think if she take Rubin in the sideshow them carnival people might try to keep him.

When you gets the town gossip talkin' about the town drunk you is goin' to hear somethin' whether you wants to or not. Miss Pinwhistle tole me she tole Otto Nelson, who you remembers is the town drunk, that if he would stop drinkin' it would lengthen his days an' she say he tole her he agree with her 'cause he was broke once an' couldn't buy a drink an' it was the longest day of his life. She also say she tole him his wife was a angel to put up with him an' she didn't know how he could live without her an' he say, "A lot cheaper."

That's all the news for now.

Cousin Hank

21

Chickpea
U.S.A.

Dear Cousin Elrod:

There ain't much news to write you as nothin' much ever seem to happen in Chickpea which is what make it such a nice place to live if you calls that livin'. Anyway, Stew Borders went to the big city an' went an' got himself helt up by some feller who pull a knife on him. Stew tole me the feller taken his ring, his watch, an' his wallet with nearly one-hunerd dollars in it. I ask Stew if he have his revolver with him which I know he carries all the time an' Stew say, "Yes. But I was lucky. The feller didn't find it."

Steve Weller's wife has got real fat from eatin' too much candy. She say she do all she can to control herself but just can't stop an' keeps on gainin' somethin' awful. Stew Borders tole her if she wants to stop eatin' candy to fill up on it an' then drink a lot of lemonade an' she'll get so sick she'll never eat no more candy. Well, Mrs. Weller she up an try this an' now she's still eatin' candy but can't stand to look at a glass of lemonade.

Pat Wilburn land in the Good Samaritan Hospital last week. It seem he has been makin' some money on the side buyin' an' sellin' use cars since he ain't been doin' too well farmin' lately. T'other day one of his mules die an' so he go over to Central City to the mule fair they has ever Tuesday to get him a mule. It seem he go aroun' lookin' at them mules this mule fair has for sale an' is so use to kickin' tires on them use cars he get carried away an' kick the left hin' leg of one of them mules an' that's how he come to be in the hospital.

It must be nice to be a Indian like Koko an' live by the sun an' the moon. T'other day I asks Koko what time it is an' he say, "It's half past somethin'."

Like I tole you in one of my letters, Doc Storkbill's office is a ideal one for a small town. You can set in his waitin' room an' hear everthin' what go on in his office an' what he say to his patients. I was settin' there with Stew Borders who was imaginin' he got somethin' wrong with him as usual an' I heared Doc tell a feller he had to quit drinkin' coffee 'cause it was a slow poison. An' this man say to Doc, "It must be a slow poison 'cause I been drinkin' it for sixty years an' it ain't kilt me yet." Later, Doc was talkin' to some woman an' she ask him, "What should I do when my baby throw up?" An' Doc tell her, "Wipe it up."

I tell you, Elrod, that Dink Porter is turnin' out to be a right smart kid. T'other day I asks him what weigh the most, a pound of feathers or a pound of lead? Natcherly, like ever-body else he say a pound of lead. When I tole him they weighs the same he look at me an' ask, "What would you rather be hit on the head with, a pound of feathers or a pound of lead?"

I meets Doc Storkbill on the street yesterday an' he look powerful upset. I asks him what is the matter an' he tole me he come real near losin' Stew Border's wife, Becky. He tole me he leave instructions with Stew for him to give her no more of a white powder than he could get on a dime an' the next morn-ing Becky was almos' dead. Doc say he ask Stew if he follow the directions he give him an' Stew say he did, but not havin' a dime he use two nickels.

Troy Conners has been workin' part time for the county in order to pick up some extra money an' was helpin' one of the men with a big tank of somethin' which blowed up. I went to see Troy in the Good Samaritan Hospital an' asks him if he was calm an' collected after the explosion an' he say he was calm but t'other feller was collected. Doc Storkbill tole me later that Troy was bust up somethin' awful an' the only difference between him an' some guy he call Humpty Dumpty was they was able to put Troy back together again, whatever he mean by that.

Arnold Dinglehoffer tole us he was eatin' lunch down at Miss Cranbock's Diner an' he heard her fussin' at the cook back in the kitchen. He low Miss Cranbock was tellin' the cook not to put so much food on the plates an' he heared her say, "We're feedin' them, not fattenin' them."

I remarks to Koko, the Indian, t'other day that I thinks it is goin' to rain an' he say it ain't. I asks him how he can tell an' he say he watch the squirrels an' if they is eatin' in the trees it mean it is goin' to rain but if they is eatin' on the ground it mean it ain't goin' to rain. I asks him, "What do it mean if half of them is eatin' in the trees an' half of them is eatin' on the ground?" An' he tole me it mean half of them is wrong.

That's all the news for now.

Cousin Hank

22

Chickpea
U.S.A.

Dear Cousin Elrod:

If I'd run into Miss Pinwhistle more often I might have more news to write you, Elrod. Sometime you get almost scairt hearin' some of the things she tell you an' then again some of them is as juicy as a overripe peach hangin' on a high limb. In fack, if you are a friend of Miss Pinwhistle you don't need to take the paper what come out of Central City an' if you know Miss Thornberry it's like havin' the Sunday supplement.

Miss Pinwhistle tole me t'other day her grandaddy tole her when she was a little girl about some man in Chickpea who had a telephone put in his house when they was first invent an' then find out with the only phone in town he don't have nobody to call up an' talk to an' that he had to wait nearly four year before somebody else get a phone an' he could use his. He also tole me, she said, that the town gossip nearly lose her mind till she get one an' could listen in an' after that he say the news really get around fast. I thought it real funny her talkin' about a town gossip what with her bein' one herself, but I guess she don't realize that, bein' like most folks who don't know what they really is.

Them folks down at Caney Church helt their annual fish fry t'other day an' it make all the fishermen who ain't members of their congregation mad as usual, this bein' 'cause everbody knows they dynamites Coon Creek to get the fish for this fish fry. They denies this, of course, what with it bein' against the law an' everthin' an' they think they is smart timin' this fish fry at the time of the year we has a lot of thunderstorms so if anybody find any fish floatin' in Coon Creek them Caney Church folks just low they was kilt by the thunder an' lightnin'. Everbody know this ain't so but we has never been able to catch them at it.

Miss Thornberry, the gossipy old school teacher who retire

some years ago seem to be still teachin', you might say. I heared her advisin' the young Kramer couple who just have their first baby that if they wants to raise it right they had better keep it away from its granparents.

Arnold Dinglehoffer had him a runt pig out of his last litter an' it was so cute he give it to Mel Thurman who taken it home an' make a pet out of it. Mel's wife, Anna, think so much of it she name it Porky an' keep it in a box next to their bed. This was okay as long as Porky stay little, but when he get big enough he is able to get out of this box by himself an' one night he must have got hungry 'cause he climb out of his box an' go out in the hallway where it is real dark an' he fall down the steps. This don't hurt him none but it scairt him a powerful lot 'cause he ain't never fall down no steps before an' Mel tole me you never hear such squealin' an' carryin' on come from that little piglet. It wake up everbody in the house an' some of them thinks the end of the world is done come. Mel want to get rid of Porky but Anna solve everthin' by gettin' a bigger box an' coverin' the top with wire mesh.

Did you hear about our state startin' up a lottery to raise money? It get under way t'other day an' most everbody run aroun' buying tickets like the lottery was goin' out of business the next day. Everbody I asks if they wins anything all tells me yes an' I figgers there is either a lot of winnin' tickets or a lot of liars in Chickpea. Doc Storkbill tole me he didn't win nothin' so I guess him an' me is the only two honest folks in Chickpea an' I ain't that sure about Doc. One lady tole me the money she win come in real handy an' I can't help but think all the money them people lose would of come in handy too. I never bought no ticket 'cause I'm so unlucky if it was rainin' soup I'd have a fork in my hand. The lottery tickets was late gettin' printed once an' Stew Borders low printin' a winnin' ticket must of bust the printin' machine. Stew also low he think folks who want to get rich from the lottery end up with lessery.

That's all the news for now.

Cousin Hank

23

Chickpea
U.S.A.

Dear Cousin Elrod:

I tell you, Elrod, it's been rainin' what they calls cats an' dogs for over a week an' you can't do nothin'. What is worse than the rain is havin' to listen to all them wiseacres sayin', "It's good for the ground water. It's good for the ground water." It's done got my nerves in a frazzle hearin' this everwhere I go an' I feels worser than a hen with a egg busted in her. T'other day Stew Borders say he need a boat instead of a tractor if he want to get his fields plow this spring. An' Arnold Dinglehoffer say he would give one-hunerd dollars just to see a handful of dust. Steve Weller up an' tell him to come down to his house an' he can see all the dust he want 'cause his wife is such a bad housekeeper. In fack, Steve say his house is so full of dust he thinks his wife is collectin' it.

We was talkin' about big cities down at the Cracker Barrel Gen. Store an' Will Garret say what he don't like about them big cities is that if you want to see a tree or some grass you has to go to a park. Ezra Moore say he feel out of place in them cities 'cause they is full of nothin' but strangers an' folks like him from a small town never meets a stranger an' he go on to say he get look at real funny ever time he try to be nice. He say he quit tryin' to speak to everbody an' start goin' aroun' with no smile on his face like everbody else he see an' he don't like it. Kelly Vance say he miss seein' real dogs 'cause them sissy city dogs is all on chains an' look like they just come from the barber shop. He low them dogs wouldn't know a rabbit if they seen one. Danny Mings say he agree with him an' add that the only birds he see in the cities is pigeons an' there is too many of them.

Elrod, there has been a heap of hexin' goin' on in Chickpea an' its environments lately. Some folks has been gettin' wreaths in their pillows an' red rings aroun' their bodies an' all sorts of peculiar things is goin' on which is the way I heared these hexes is suppose to work an' all this is suppose to be due to somebody puttin' the hex on you. This hexin' is done by folks who is cowards an' is afeared to punch somebody in the nose so they lets it get out that a hex is on somebody an' this seems to get that somebody all work up an' real nervous. Anyways this hexin' sure do scare folks what hear a hex is put on them an' they gets sick an' I even hear sometime they dies. Personally, I don't believe in such hokum an' neither do most folks aroun' here. Now that Koko is a real smart Indian. When this hexin' business start up he lets it get knowed that he has some powerful medicine what can keep any hex from workin' an' folks that is hexed lines up in front of his shack. Koko charge good money for this medicine an' I guess he figger if a person is dumb enough to fall for a hex he is dumb enough to pay to get rid of it.

You remember that Mr. Winterbottom I tell you about who claim he is so smart he never fall for no foolishness or superstition? Well somebody want to play a joke on him an' tole him they heared a hex is out on him. Old Winterbottom just laugh an' say, "So what." He say he don't pay no heed to such stuff an' that it don't bother him none at all. That night some fellers follow him an' sees him sneak in Koko's shack an' we all know it is to get some of Koko's strong medicine. But nobody ever tole Winterbottom this 'cause they feels they done enough to him already.

T'other day I was standin' on the street talkin' to Rubin Flener when I meets a feller by name of Joe Thurman who is visitin' his brother Mel Thurman who is the guard at the prison over in Central City. This Joe Thurman is a stranger in Chickpea never havin' been here before but he know me 'cause Mel has already interduce us. But he don't know who Rubin is an' so I interduce him. This Joe is real friendly like an' he talk a lot about politics an' other interestin' subjects. Rubin of course don't have nothin' to say as usual an' just stand there noddin' his head like he is agreein' with everthin' Joe Thurman is sayin'.

When Rubin leave, Joe say to me, "Now there is a real smart feller an' a good talker too." I didn't have the heart to tell him Rubin is the village idiot which is why he just nod his head an' say nothin'. All this remind me of what I heared Plato had say years ago which is that no one is more smart than the person who agree with you.

That's all the news for now.

Cousin Hank

24

Chickpea
U.S.A.

Dear Cousin Elrod:

Thank you for your last letter an' lettin' me know everthin' is goin' all right with you.

There ain't much happen here lately except you remember old Doc Storkbill? Well, old Doc always recommend his son's funeral parlor to the families of those folks he don't cure an' this make Gilmore powerful mad. Gilmore run his funeral parlor here in Chickpea for over forty year an' miss the business Doc use to send him an' he show it an' this cause a lot of bad blood between him an' Doc. In the old days I think this would of end up in a dool between them but bein' civilize all they does is go aroun' an' say bad things about one n'tother.

Now mentionin' them remind me of the time I went to Gilmore's funeral parlor when they was buryin' Otto Nelson who everbody call the town drunk. I didn't know Otto too well but I likes to pay my respecks to the dead an' besides outside of drinkin' almost all the time I never heared of Otto doin' anythin' real bad an' I never knowed of him to have kilt nobody neither. The only trouble I ever heared of him bein' in was with the IRS when he try to claim Larry Blumer who run the Lion's Den Saloon as a dependent on his income tax on account of he spend so much money there he support him. Otto look real nice the day they bury him an' if Gilmore hadn't cover up his red nose he would of look just like I remembers him. Reverend Tatum who haven't been in Chickpea long enough to know Otto start the service with a eulogy an' say such nice things about Otto that some of his relatives gets up an' leaves thinkin' they is at the wrong funeral.

Koko was complainin' to me about how bad some of the pale face folks in Chickpea treats him an' he say it is on account of he is a foreigner. I tole him he ain't no foreigner, but is one of the original Americans. He look at me an' say, "When you is the only one you is a foreigner."

I drop in on Stew Borders t'other day after I heared he is sick an' I fine him standin' in his bedroom a shakin' an' a tremlin' somethin' awful. I asks him what is the matter with him an' he say Doc Storkbill give him some medicine an' on the bottle it say to shake before takin'.

You know how it is when you is sick an' think you is dyin'? Well, old Gilmore who been mad at Doc Storkbill ever since Doc's son open a funeral parlor in Chickpea an' give him competition has been goin' to a doctor in Central City ever since even if it mean travelin' there ever time he feel bad. Well, t'other night he get real sick an' think he is dyin' an' want to get right with the Lord an' everbody in Chickpea as well, so he ask his wife to call Doc Storkbill an' tell him he forgives him an' will Doc come over an' save him. So Mary gets Doc Storkbill on the phone an' tell him Leviticus is at death's door an' will he come over an' pull him through?

I run into Stew Borders on Main Street an' he was wearin' a tolerable nice sweater which he tole me is made out of more hair which he say come from a Angora cat. I didn't want to embarrass him or I would have tole him he mean a Angola goat.

Ever time Tink Collins go in an' out of Miss Cranbock's Diner he leave the door open an' she get real mad especially in the summertime when he lets all the flies in. It get right amusin' to everbody when he do this an' she yell at him, "What the matter with you? You live on a hill?"

Stew Borders is always whistlin' or singin' or doin' somethin' to make a noise which is usually annoyin' to most everbody an' t'other day he was whistlin' up a tune somethin' awful an' I asks him the name of it an' he tole me it is a tune name of Sweet Sue. I asks him who writ it an' he low he don't know but it must of been writ by a lawyer.

Before I closes I wants to tell you about meetin' Miss Thornberry who is with some feller she interduce me to by name of Dean Thackery. When I meet them they is usin' such big words I think they is talkin' in a foreign language. After talkin' to this Mr. Thackery for a few minutes I can tell he don't know nothin' about farmin' or plantin' by the signs or huntin' an' fishin'. He is one of them eddycated fools what drops in on Chickpea ever now an' then. Also I later learns Dean ain't his first name but is somethin' he is call because he is connect with a college.

That's all the news for now.

Cousin Hank

25

Chickpea
U.S.A.

Dear Cousin Elrod:

As you knows I still wants you to come back to Chickpea to live after you retires. I believes the Devil give us our cities but I thanks the Lord for givin' us our small towns where a human bein' can live the way he is suppose to. In a small town you has a lot of friends for the simple reason you is one yourself. An' all the window boxes an' flower pots in the big cities can't beat one garden in your backyard where you is with God ever time you works in it. You just got to come back to Chickpea, Elrod. That's all there is to it.

I been afraid we was goin' to have us a feud here in Chickpea. It seem Luke Porter bought his son, Dink, a drum an' the youngun like to of wore out the ears on old man Zigart who live next door to them. T'other day Mr. Zigart ask Dink if he knowed what was inside the drum an' that's when the trouble start.

Yesterday they had to call Doc Storkbill to come revive Miss Pinwhistle. She look out her window an' see a raccoon lookin' in an' think it's a burglar an' she faint plumb unconscious.

Speakin' of Doc Storkbill remind me of when Stew Borders ask me to go with him to see Doc when his artheritis start actin' up, him bein' too much of a coward to go alone. Doc Storkbill write him out a perscription an' say this'll be good for your artheritis and Stew look at him an' say, "Don't give me something good for my artheritis. It don't need no help. Give me somethin' good for me." It embarrass me to be with him when he say such a dumb thing.

Stew Borders tell me he was in a place called a Art Museum once an' he saw a concrete head on a post with a sign that said 'Bust by some guy with a Greek name.' He say he's glad they knowed who bust it 'cause they might of blame it on him. And then Arnold Dinglehoffer who was listenin' up an' lowed them folks who run them museums must be mighty careless 'cause half of what he ever see in them places was busted.

Jason Gump who run the feed store had to go to New York on business an' he taken his wife along. They goes by bus to Central City an' gets on one of them airyplanes to fly to New York. Jason been drinkin' an' when he set down in the plane he fall asleep. When he wake up he look out the window an' start hollerin', "The propellers done fell off!" It take three men to hole him down while his wife explain they is on one of them jet airyplanes what don't have no propellers. They say she is real embarrass by the way he act.

We have a big argumint at the Cracker Barrel Gen. Store when Stew Borders say you can go to Europe by train. When we tell him he is nuts he say Mrs. Winterbottom, who is always gettin' seasick, tole his wife the last time she go to Europe was by rail.

There ain't much other news to write about excep' Craig Jamison who has been tryin' to sell them pretty pitchers he paints of scenes aroun' Chickpea finally sell a pitcher for five-hunerd dollars. It seem some art man from the big city get steer over to see what Craig was paintin' but when he look at them pretty pitchers he tole Craig they pretty good but nobody'll want to buy them. This make Craig feel real bad, but on his way out the art man see a piece of paper with all kinds of pretty paint smear over it an' he told Craig it is a beautiful piece of modern art. The man taken it with him an' in a few days he send Craig a check for five-hunerd dollars after he taken out what he call his commission. Craig say he is scairt to tell the art man that piece of paper was what he clean his brushes on 'cause the art man might want his money back. Now Craig paint nothin' but blobs and send it to the art man who tole him he is doin' real good an' will make a lot of money as a artist.

I was shoppin' in the Cracker Barrel Gen. Store t'other day an' I asks West Bennet for five pig's feet an' that smart aleck tole me he only had four 'cause that's all the feet the pig had. After he saw how disappointed I was he say he just jokin' an' give me the five I asks for. It make me so mad that if I wasn't gettin' these pig's feet for company I was havin' over I would have walk out.

We was discussin' horses t'other day an' I ask what a quarter horse was an' Travis Wilson up an' lows he reckon it's a horse with two-bits in its mouth.

Before I closes, I was wonderin' if you went out an' look at the eclipse of the sun we had t'other day. Folks in Chickpea gets real excited about it an' them what didn't get scairt an' think it was the end of the world comin' smoked glass so they could watch it. While it was goin' on Caney Church had a special service for them what was scairt. Dink ask his mother if he could go out an' watch it an' she say he could but not to get too close to it.

That's all the news for now.

Cousin Hank

26

Chickpea
U.S.A.

Dear Cousin Elrod:

One time I gets to talkin' to Koko after he have a drink or
two an' he was in a real mellow mood which is the state he
get to before the whoopin' an' hollerin' state an' I asks him
how he come to be in Chickpea which is a powerful long way
from the reservation he talk about growin' up on. Koko look
rather sad when I asks this an' he say he ain't never tole
nobody an' if I promise to keep it to myself he will tell me.
When I tole this old Indian his secret will be safe with me he
say, "Many moons ago I live on the reservation with my
people an' I fall in love with a beautiful maiden name of
Little Moon who is as sweet an' innocent as any Indian
maiden can be. She love me too an' we make much plans to
have our future together an' raise many papoose. But there is
a brave in our tribe name of Big Black Bear an' he taken Little
Moon away one night by force an' nobody know where they
go. Almost a year later I gets a letter from Little Moon tellin'
me where to find her an' sayin' Big Black Bear has keep her a
prisoner an' treat her somethin' awful. She say he beat her an'
their papoose an' she beg me to come save her. I sets out
immediate an' heads for the little town Big Black Bear has got
her in an' I finds the house where she live. I likes to die when
I see her she look so bad her face all swole an' bruise from
bein' beat up an' she is holdin' a tiny papoose what look like it
never have nothin' to eat. I asks her why she don't run away
an' she say Big Black Bear say he will hunt her down an' kill
her if she do an' will then kill some of her relatives too so she
is afraid not just for herself but for them others as well 'cause
Big Black Bear is real mean an' she knows he will do what he
say. I tries to comfort her for a while as best I can an' when I
looks at the papoose again I sees it is dead an' that evenin'

Little Moon she die too. So I sets there an' waits for Big Black Bear to come home an' after he do I waits until it get good an' dark before I leaves. I thinks it best not to go back to the reservation 'cause they all knows I was goin' to find Little Moon so I walks into the woods an' keeps goin' till I gets to this place which is many moons ago. This is a nice place then. Circle City ain't as big as Chickpea is now an' there weren't no Chickpea then. But there was plenty game in woods an' much fish in creek. It stay like that till white man ruin it." This end what he have to say an' I feels right bad after hearin' it an' tole Koko I got to go. Besides he been drinkin' while he talk an' it look like he gettin' close to the whoopin' an' hollerin' stage an' while I thinks he is harmless I don't feel like takin' no chances.

A insurance man come to Chickpea an' try to sell Stew Borders a health insurance policy. He say older folks don't know what coverage they will need an' Stew tell him that is easy to know 'cause it is always the one you don't have when you needs it most, an' it probably be a burial policy anyways.

Some feller land one of them little airyplanes on Kelly Vance's farm an' takes folks up in the air for two dollars a ride. Nearly everbody in Chickpea take advantage of this chance to ride in a airyplane except Glave Robards who say he ain't lost nothin' up there but I think he just plain scairt. Stew Borders taken a ride an' this airyplane driver decide to have a little fun with him an' he fly upside down an' do loops an' all kinds of crazy things. Stew tole me later the airyplane man say to him, "I bet half the people on the ground thought we was goin' to crash an' get kilt." Stew tole me he tole the airyplane man half the people in the airyplane thought so too.

Folks has been after Miss Cranbock to get her to start givin' credit again, but she say she is finally gettin' to make money at her diner an' she ain't about to stop a good thing when she got it goin'. One thing I will say about her, Elrod, an' that is she ain't as hardhearted as folks makes her out 'cause many a time I see her put extra food on a plate if her customer look poor an' hungry an' she never turn no begger away from her back door.

That's all the news for now.

Cousin Hank

27

Chickpea
U.S.A.

Dear Cousin Elrod:

Stew Borders is almost as bad a gossip as Miss Pinwhistle an' t'other day he get wound up an' tole me about what happen in Chickpea a long time ago when he was a youngun. I growed up here like he did but I never remember what he tole me ever happenin' so I don't know if he make it up or what. Anyways, he say when he was little, a man by name of Thompson rent out his pasture to one of them travelin' carnivals so they could set up operations for a few days an' it seem this carnival don't do too well an' instead of gettin' money this Thompson feller has to take a llama for his rent which Stew say Thompson seem glad to do as no one in Chickpea ever has a llama before which he say is a animal what come from South America. For about six months folks come out to his place to see this llama an' then the interest die down an' about a year later so does the llama which Thompson find dead in his barn one morning from what seem natural causes. Now accordin' to Stew Borders this Thompson ain't one to take a loss on nothin' so he run around real fast an' raffles off his llama at two dollars a chance an' the first day he sell a great many tickets. In fack, he do so well he has the drawin' the next day in the town square 'cause he's afeared the sheriff or somebody might look into things. Well, some feller have the winnin' ticket an' all the rest of the folks who lose goes home an' Thompson takes the winnin' feller out to his farm to pick up his llama. Thompson go in his barn an' then come right out an' tole the feller, "Your llama just drop dead," an give the feller his two dollars back which satisfy him. I ask Stew if Thompson give everbody their money back an' he say no 'cause Thompson claim they didn't have nothin' to complain about since they losers.

Stew Borders an' his wife taken a trip out west in their autymobile an' since they get back it is all he talk about. I don't see his wife very much but I guess it's all she talk about too. Stew say he is real disappointed in seein' a lot of them places he read about. He say the Grand Canyon is nothin' but a big ditch with a lot of water runnin' through it but it's so far down you can't hardly see it. He say he see a lot of Indians out west but none of them knowed Koko an' he say he ask ever one he could talk to. He say what he didn't like about the west was that the distances is so far apart he nearly run out of gas a couple of times. He say he get to the Pacific Ocean an' that you can't tell it from the Atlantic Ocean which he seen once when he was in Atlantic City. He tole me he guess all them men what make the west so interestin' is dead now an' he never seen a cowboy with a gun on his hip neither. He go on to say that after drivin' all them miles Chickpea sure did look good to him. He say the most of which you see out west except some mountains which gets in your way is sky. I meets Miss Thornberry after Stew has been tellin' her about his trip an' she say Stew ain't got no soul or imagination an' don't appreciate nothin'. She might be right but Stew do seem to appreciate Chickpea, but then again that don't take no imagination. Arnold Dinglehoffer agree with Stew an' say he can do all the travelin' he want in his rockin' chair. Dinglehoffer also say he don't like to take no trips in his autymobile 'cause to get anywhere you has to drive fast an' he don't like to drive fast. Somebody once say about Dinglehoffer's drivin' that if he went any slower he'd back into somethin'.

That's all the news for now.

Cousin Hank

P.S. T'other day I was walkin' on the street with Stew Borders an' we meets a stranger what turn out to be a feller visitin' Pat

Wilburn. We gets to talkin' an' he ask if any big men was ever borned in Chickpea an' Stew tole him, "No, only little babies."

28

Chickpea
U.S.A.

Dear Cousin Elrod:

You remember, Elrod, when we was young an' use to help our daddies in the fields we'd see one of them phantom rains an' watch that rain fall out of them clouds an' never hit the earth? Well, that fool Stew Borders seen one of them t'other day an' run aroun' scarin' everbody yellin' a tornado is comin'. I tole this to our County Agent who is a right smart feller name of Arthur Singer who tole me this happen once in a while if the feller seein' it ain't familiar with phantom rain which he tole me is called Virga. But it's hard for me to understand how Stew who growed up farmin' can make such a dumb mistake an' he do things like this all the time. Folks say if he ever see a real tornado he won't recognize it an' if he do nobody'll believe him. I use to think he was harmless but now I ain't so sure an' am afeared he can be downright dangerous. He is always tellin' folks what to do an' how to save money treatin' themselfs when they feels poorly. Evan Stillwell once tell him it is a shame him wastin' his medical degree by bein' a farmer. An' Stew took this as a compliment. Just t'other day Stew have everbody in Chickpea breakin' out in a cole sweat tellin' them Doc Storkbill tole him he was goin' to retire. But it seem Doc Storkbill had mean he was just turnin' in for the night an' Stew get mix up as usual. I think the only reason Stew ain't been sue is 'cause he ain't got nothin' if you win.

We almost gets us another town drunk in Chickpea. Troy Conners is goin' aroun' all the time half drunk. One day Will Garret ask him why he always stay half drunk an' Troy tell him he ain't got enough money to get drunk. Will Garret has a habit of askin' people all kind of personal questions an' once he ask Jerry Blumer who run the Lions Den Saloon why he don't drink an' Jerry tell him the stuff was made to sell not to buy.

Arnold Dinglehoffer say he tell me somethin' if I promise I won't spread it around but when he was a little boy Stew Borders' folks taken him to the big city an' they went in a place call a zoo which Stew tole us boys is where a lot of animals is lock up like they is commit a crime or somethin'. He say some is wearin' stripes like the prisoners at the penitentiary at Central City an' they would be easy to catch if they was to escape. He also tole us he seen a big animal call a elefant which have a tail at each end of its body. He also tole us a lot of lies about a place he went to call a circus an' expect us to believe him when he say there is men there what fly through the air an' catch themselfs on swings. Us younguns knowed he was lyin' 'cause men can't fly 'cause they ain't got no wings. An' when Stew tole us they shoot some feller out of a canon clear across a big room made out of a tent we quits speakin' to him an' treats him somethin' awful for a long time. But like I asks you, don't say I ever tell you this 'cause some of them fellers what didn't believe Stew is still ashame of themselfs an' we all sometime wonder if this might not have somethin' to do with the way he act today. Anyway this is what Arnold says.

We was settin' down at the Cracker Barrel Gen. Store t'other day talkin' as usual an' somebody ask West Bennet, "If the world is gettin' smaller as they been sayin', how come the postage rates ain't gettin' cheaper?"

Elrod, that Winterbottom feller is still gettin' on everbody's nerves what with him knowin' it all an' never lowin' to a mistake ever. To give you a example of what I means for instance t'other day down at the Cracker Barrel Gen. Store someone say he read all about a big earthquake what kill a lot of folks down in Mexico an Winterbottom say, "I knowed it would."

It look like all I does these days is go to the Good Samaritan Hospital to see folks what is sick or injure. This time I visits Sam Miller's daughter, Dorothy, who is bust up somethin' awful. It seems she just graduate from high school last week an' is so use to havin' all them autymobiles stop when she get on an' off them school buses that when she taken a bus to Central City for the first time she get off an' walk in front of a auto which she think is goin' to stop for her but it don't. If they is goin' to eddycate kids they ought to at least teach them how to cross the street.

That's all the news for now.

Cousin Hank

29

Chickpea
U.S.A.

Dear Cousin Elrod:

I has a little pain t'other day, Elrod, an' I go to have Doc Storkbill take a look at me an' it turn out to be nothin' at all just somethin' I must have eat at Miss Cranbock's Diner which ain't unusual. Anyways, while I is settin' there I listens to all them ladies which is also waitin' to see Doc about their ailments which is mostly cause by their husbands. An' speakin' of husbands that's all they seems to talk about. Mrs. Crump was sayin' they is broke all the time 'cause Jethro spend all his money makin' a show so folks will think they is rich which they ain't. She also say Jethro is a optimist 'cause when she ask him to do somethin' around the house he always say, "I'll do it tomorrow when I'm feelin' better." She go on to say if folks hires somebody to do some housework an' such they calls them a maid, but she do it for nothin' an' she is call a wife. I would have like to of hear more of this but Doc sticks his head out of his office an' tell me to come in. All Doc do is take a lot of time givin' me a diet. He could of save time by just tellin' me to eat what I don't like.

Later that day I was down at the Cracker Barrel Gen. Store

tellin' the fellers what I hear them ladies say an' how I learn a lot listenin' to them. Stew Borders say he learn a lot after he marry but then it was too late. Evan Stillwell up an' say this remind him of a feller who marry a rich lady for her money an' then find out he could of borrow it cheaper. Somebody ask why Miss Pinwhistle never marry an' Stew Borders low it is probably 'cause she never find a feller smart enough to have make a lot of money an' dumb enough to ask her to marry him.

I met Rubin, the village idiot, t'other day standin' on the side of the main road that run from Chickpea to Central City an' stops an' talks to him a spell. While we is talkin' a big autymobile drive up an' stop an' a feller ask us, "How do you get to Central City from here?" Before I could tell him, Rubin he walk up to this autymobile an' take his hat off real perlite like which is the way his mother teach him an' he say to this feller, "I always gets there by bus myself."

Stew Borders is one of them fellers what is always playin' a practical joke on folks an' then laughin' up a storm at their misery. Well, lately he has been interducin' Becky as his first wife an' this has got her nearly plumb upset. She talk this over one day with Miss Thornberry who tell her to interduce Stew as her first husband an' see how he like it. Now Becky can't wait till she can do this an' one day on leavin' church with Stew she see a friend of hers with a lady she don't know so she say hello to her friend an' then interduces Stew to this other lady as her first husband an' Stew he don't like it a bit an' don't seem to think it funny at all. In fack, he get so mad he is fit to be tie an' he get so red in the face everbody think he is havin' a seizure. But it sure work 'cause he never interduce Becky like that again.

One day I'm settin' in Doc Storkbill's office with Stew who is imaginin' he has some terrible disease or somethin' which I knows he don't have but is just imaginin' it again like he do ever now an' then. I tell you, Elrod, if Stew ever read one of them medical books like sends Luke Porter, the real estate man, to see Doc ever time he read it I am afraid it will prove fatal. Now while we is settin' there Doc rushes out of his office an' after tellin' everbody not to get well while he is gone he say, "Just set there for a short spell. Jethro Crump just call an' say his wife is gettin' ready to have her baby an' I will hurry as fast as I can." So everbody sets there real patient like an' Doc he ain't gone very long 'cause he know his waitin' room is full of folks who needs him real bad. He comes rushin' back in an' somebody ask him if it is a boy or a girl an' without slowin' up Doc say he don't know he was in too big of a hurry to look.

That's all the news for now.

Cousin Hank

P.S. Think some more of what I writ you about comin' back to Chickpea after you retires.

30

Chickpea
U.S.A.

Dear Cousin Elrod:

Somethin' happen one day quite a long spell ago an' I never dare tell nobody about it an' I wants you to tear this letter up after you reads it an' then I wants you to keep the contents to yourself. It so happen I was takin' one of my constitution walks one evenin' an' I happens to go past Koko's shack an' I sees a great big feller wearin' one of them big hats like you hears about folks wearin' out west an' he is knockin' up a storm on Koko's door. Now I knowed Koko was in Central City visitin' a friend an' that he was due to get back home real soon so I goes over real friendly like we are in Chickpea to tell this feller if he wait a short spell Koko will be back. I calls out a hello to this feller an' when he turn around I see a great big star on his chest what say U.S. Marshal an' when I looks at his car which he park nearby I see it has got New Mexico license plates on it. Of course this shake me up a bit 'cause I remember what Koko once tell me about Little Moon an' Big Black Bear an' I knowed even if it did happen many years ago some folks never gives up lookin' for somebody if they wants them bad enough.

So I holds my tongue an' don't volunteer no information which is always the smart thing to do anyways. I just ask this Marshal feller if I can be of any help to him an' he say he is lookin' for a Indian name of Koko who is suppose to live here an' do I know where he is. My mind start movin' real fast an' I tole him Koko is out of town an' won't be back till tomorrow. So this feller thank me an' say he will come back tomorrow an' he drive away. I sets down after he is out of sight an' sure enough in about a hour here come Koko, walkin' as spry as a teenager in spite of his some ninety years. I tole him about this Marshal feller an' he look real scairt. I tole him not to worry, that I been thinkin' an' for him to come home with me an' do what I tells him to do. I gets him settle in my house an' tole him not to leave for any reason a-tall an' stay put until I returns which won't be until the next day. Koko promise me he will do what I says an' I am sure he will, as scairt as he is. Then I drives to Central City an' buys what is call makeup an' a bottle of black hair dye an' drives back to Koko's place an' parks my car out of sight. I slept there that night an' in the mornin' I gets up real early an' puts on some of Koko's clothes which fits me tolerable well an' then I sets down an' waits for that Marshal feller to come back like he say he will. I don't have to wait long before I hears a car drive up an' then a knockin' on the door. I gets up an feels real confident the Marshal feller won't recognize me what with all the copper makeup an' my blond hair all black. I opens the door an' sure enough there is this Marshal feller just like he say he'll be. The only thing what worries me is my blue eyes but if he say anythin' I plan on tellin' him I is a half-breed. But the Marshal feller don't recognize me an' he say he want to see Koko. I tells him I am Koko an' he say, "You is too young to be Koko." So I says, "Oh. You mean old Koko, my father, who come here many moons ago but who is dead now for ten year." When I says this the Marshal feller takes a piece of paper out of his pocket which say warrant an' I sees him write across this the word deceased. He look at me an' say, "Well, that saves the state a lot of trouble an' money." He thank me an' drive off an' we never sees him again.

That's all the news for now.

Cousin Hank

31

Chickpea
U.S.A.

Dear Cousin Elrod:

I enjoy very much your last letter an' in reply to your askin' me if my friend appreciate what I do for him I am glad to report that he appreciate it very much. But first let me thank you for not mentionin' his name in case your letter fall into other hands. In fack, Elrod, Koko appreciate too much what I do for him. The first thing he do after I go back home with all my make up wash off an' my hair blond again an' tell him he can go home is he cuts his arm an' then cuts mine an' rubs the wounds together an' say we is now blood brothers. An' he is still bringin' me game an' cuttin' my grass an' not lettin' me pay him an' all this embarrass me very much but there is nothin' I can do about it an' it seem to make him very happy.

It has been a bad spring here this year, Elrod. One day it is so hot you can't hardly stand it an' the next day it is so cold you nearly freezes yourself to death. It is like I hear Plato who live in Chickpea years ago is suppose to have say about such weather an' that is you should be real comfortable on such days 'cause the temperatures averages out to a real comfortable mean temperature. I will say this, it sure is a mean temperature all right. It is like havin' your head in a oven an' your feet in a ice box an' expectin' to have a comfortable average temperature. Personally, it don't make no sense to me.

Speakin' of the weather remind me that a lot of folks go to Koko, the Indian, to ask him what the weather will be 'cause they believes Indians knows all about such nature things. Koko he been lookin' at the sky an' furrowin' his brow an' tellin' everbody for weeks it is goin' to rain the next day an' it don't. Someone ask him what is the matter he can't do no better than them fellers on TV an' he say real wise like, "In dry weather all signs fail."

I asks Henry Estes t'other day if he ever win in the lottery since it come out an' he ask me if I am crazy or somethin' thinkin' a retire school teacher livin' on a little pension have any money for such foolishness. I reminds him I once hear him say he like to gamble an' he say a man on a diet like to eat, too. He go on to say he gamble this way—an' that is doin' what he call bet against himself. He tole me he go to the races once in a while an' picks a horse but don't bet on it an' if it lose he say he win two dollars. I asks him, "What if it win?" An' Henry say, "If it win an' pay five to one I figgers I loses ten dollars. But it don't take me long not bettin' to get even again." I don't tell him but I thinks he is a little nuts doin' this but if it make him happy I guess it is okay an' beside he might just have somethin' goin' for him, at that. Leastways when he lose his money he get to keep it.

Leviticus Gilmore's wife is so ugly it make folks who see her real sad an' when there ain't enough mournin' goin' on at his funeral parlor Leviticus ask Mary to mingle with the family an' friends of the decease an' the mournin' usually pick up considerable.

You writ me how hot it is in Chicago. Well it must be hotter than that here in Chickpea an' on top of that it is the humidity which has got the women nearly crazy 'cause it take a day for clothes to dry after they washes them. It is like swimmin' when you takes a walk an' if this humidity don't let up we is all goin' to have to grow gills if we is goin' to make it. Miss Thornberry, the retire school teacher who take all them intellectual magazines tole me people is descend from animules what once live in the sea an' I tole her I think we is goin' back to the old ways if it don't start to dry up real soon. Anyways, Miss Thornberry was goin' around not long ago quotin' a magazine articule about some feller name of Darwin who low we comes from monkeys an' now she is tellin' us we is come from somethin' that must have been a fish if it live in the sea so I guesses even if she is a retire school teacher she don't know so much or else she done forget it.

That's all the news for now.

Cousin Hank

32

Chickpea
U.S.A.

Dear Cousin Elrod:

I go to Miss Cranbock's Diner with Stew Borders t'other day to eat lunch an' he look at a item she call Today's Special an' say it cost too much. Miss Cranbock tole him she got some of last weeks Special left an' it is a lot cheaper if he want to take a chance on it. Elrod, Stew is not only the cheapest but he is also the laziest feller I knows. Yesterday I was out to his place an' find him standin' an' lookin' at some seeds he was goin' to plant as if they was goin' to plant theyselfs. His bein' lazy must be catchin' 'cause he got the leanest hogs of anybody around. They is so lazy they is always leanin' against the barn or a fence.

Some lady from the big city stop in West Bennet's Cracker Barrel Gen. Store an' want to buy some meat. She get to complainin' all of West's meat is too fat an' she want some lean meat. She is fussin' so much West tole her to go out to Stew Borders' farm an' get him to sell her some fresh meat which he is sure will satisfy her 'cause Stew is so tight he feed his animals as little as possible an' they has hardly no fat on them a-tall. It seem while this lady was out there she ask Stew's wife if she have any antiques for sale an' before Becky can answer the lady Stew say, "No. We is all out but if you tells me what you wants in the line of a antique I'll be glad to make it for you." This upset the lady, but Stew's wife she save the day by tellin' the lady Stew mean he will make her a reproduction. All of which go to prove what I thinks all along, Elrod, an' that is that women is smarter then men. I wouldn't be about to say this down to the Cracker Barrel Gen. Store 'cause them fellers would run me plumb out of there. So I keeps my mouth shut which is the way everbody's mouth ought to be anyways. I knows I couldn't get away with sayin' somethin' like that to them fellers who done spend most of their lives lookin' over the back of a pair of mules while they is plowin' their fields an' such an' thinkin' they is so smart Eve never could of made them eat the apple. Anyways, it is always the wives what makes their husband buy a tractor against his will an' then can't ever get him down off it after he get it. Stew Borders finally gets him a tractor but say the only thing he don't like about it is it don't give him no manure like his mules did.

One thing I will say for Stew Borders is he is real patriotic an' loyal to Chickpea an' brag it is the only town he was ever borned in. He get madder than anybody else when them folks in Central City gets uppity over havin' them one-way streets an' one of them tells Stew Chickpea is so small it have to share Rubin, the village idiot, with Ball Town down the highway. Stew tole me he tole this feller that ain't so an' also that them one-way streets don't mean nothin' no how 'cause you can't drive but one way at a time anyways.

Miss Cranbock try out new dishes at her diner now an' then an' t'other day she make what is call a open sanwidge which don't have no bread on top an' this save her some money. She call this sanwidge the Chickpea Open an' put a big sign out in front of the restaurant to this effeck. This sign ain't been up very long when a couple of stranger fellers walks in an' ask if anybody can enter the Chickpea Open thinkin' it is a golf tournament.

While I was eatin' in the diner t'other evenin' some members of the Caney Church comes in an' asks Miss Cranbock for a donation an' she ask if they will take her donation on credit like they has been askin' her to give them dead beat customers who don't pay their bills. This make them members mad an' they walks out. Meanwhile, the customer settin' at a table next to me call Miss Cranbock an' tell her his coffee is cold, an' that he ask for a hot cup of coffee. Miss Cranbock puts her hand around the cup an' say, "The cup's hot just like you ask for."

That's all the news for now.

Cousin Hank

33

Chickpea
U.S.A.

Dear Cousin Elrod:

I tell you, Elrod, it sure is nice to hear you is gettin' ready to retire. An' it further please me to learn you might move to Chickpea when you does. Your old room is still here waitin' for you an' so is the rest of the house which I am glad to share with you. Let me know as soon as you makes up your mind what you is goin' to do.

I hates to write you somethin' like this but that Stew Borders who will say anything about anybody make a remark about Miss Pinwhistle who I do admit talk a lot about everbody. He say t'other day down at the Cracker Barrel Gen. Store that when she die her tongue will be the last thing to stop movin'. After he make me mad sayin' a thing like this about a lady just 'cause she talk a lot he stop by my house an' make me mad again. I just gets through paintin' my screen door when he walk in. Now Stew will believe anythin' you tells him but when I tole him I just paint the screen door he have to touch it. It seem he want to tell me somethin' an' he get to talkin' so fast he begin sayin' things he ain't thought of yet.

We was talkin' about ugly folks down at the Cracker Barrel Gen. Store an' Stew Borders low his wife have a sister what is about the ugliest person he ever see in all his borned days. He say if Becky's sister walk past a clock she might not stop it but she would put it on slow time an' this save her a lot of trouble when you has to set your clocks back an' forth on account of this daylight savin' time which was pass for them golfer fellers an' which plumb mess up farmin'. Stew say this sister-in-law of his has got a nose so big that when she go anywhere it always get there before her an' that her ears sticks out so she can't walk against the wind but if the wind is blowin' from behind her she go real fast. Stew say nothin' about her seem made right, an' where other girls has curves she have angles.

Steve Weller is worry about his wife who Doc Storkbill say has got very close veins an' he don't know if Doc mean they is too close together or very close to the skin. He tole us he is goin' to another doctor an' get what he call a second opinion. Stew Borders upset him when he ask him, "If this second opinion is different, which opinion is you goin' to believe?"

It has been so hot here lately all the creeks is dryin' up an' somebody say if you wants to go fishin' you has to take your own water. Stew Borders low if it get any hotter his chickens will be layin' hard boil eggs. He went on fussin', this time about prices goin' up so much it cost too much to stay alive. He is so cheap, Elrod, if it cost money to get well he would be the sickest man in Chickpea. He went to Chicago once on a convention an' when somebody say as they gets off the plane that the airport is Chicago's front porch, Stew ask, "Where is the washing machine?"

On my way home I runs into Rev. Tatum an' we gets to talkin', him doin' most of it an' he gets to remarkin' about Miss Pinwhistle an' her talkin' a whole lot about everbody an' he remark she don't believe everthin' she hear like Stew Borders do but she repeat it. An' he also say if you go to Doc Storkbill let him think you is poor an' he will cure you quicker. I am beginnin' to think Rev. Tatum is as big a gossip as the folks he talk about.

Yesterday I passes by where Koko live an' he is sunnin'

himself out in front of his shack an' I stops to talk with him a spell an' he tole me that when white man come here the Indians was doin' a powerful good job of runnin' the country. He say the huntin' an' fishin' was good an' the air was clean an' the water was so pure you could breathe an' drink without havin' to go to the doctor. He say there weren't no taxes an' other laws to keep you from enjoyin' life an' the squaws did all the work. An', he adds, white man think he can improve on this.

T'other day I was talkin' to West Bennet who run the Cracker Barrel Gen. Store in what he call the Federal Building an' I asks him, "Why do Mr. Clancy, the railroad engineer, buy all them candy bars which I sees him doin' all the time?" An' West tole me that Clancy taken them with him in the cab of his locomotive an' throwed them out to the children what is standin' along the tracks an' wavin' to him out in the country. He say he growed up on a farm an' never had much of them good kind of things give to him an' he want to make them farm kids happy if he can. I bet you don't have no bus drivers in the city doin' somethin' like that. Of course, I realizes it ain't practical to do somethin' like this in the city. But that is just what I likes about a small town, Elrod, you can do things that ain't practical nowhere else. You keep this in mind when you makes your decision on what you is goin' to do when you retires.

That's all the news for now.

Cousin Hank

34

Chickpea
U.S.A.

Dear Cousin Elrod:

I tell you, Elrod, it's like that Stew Borders is always sayin', "What you sees when you ain't got a gun." T'other day I was walkin' down that little lane that run behind our house an'

don't lead nowhere an' I sees a strange lookin' animule what
has a head like a pipe or somethin'. When I gets up to it I sees
it is a groundhog which has got his head stuck in a big tin can.
Now I knowed if I tries to pull this tin can off his head that
groundhog might scratch an' chew me up somethin' awful an'
I ain't about to get scratch an' chew up. While I'm wonderin'
what to do two young farm boys drives up in a rusty
autymobile what don't look no better than the tin can what
has got this groundhog all mess up. They looks at this critter
an' asks me, "What kind of a animule is that?" Can you
believe that, Elrod? Two farm boys who don't know what a
groundhog is even if it is wearin' a big tin can on its head. No
wonder so much livestock get shot when huntin' season is on.
Well anyways, I finally decides what to do about this critter
an' I takes a holt of that tin can with both hands an' swings
that groundhog around till he fly plumb out'n that big tin can
an' hit the ground runnin'.

You know what, Elrod? That false preacher, Sister Kaye, I
been tellin' you about who had all them ladies talkin' in tongues
an' takin' communion in her church made out of concrete
blocks while their husbands was takin' a stronger kind of
communion down at the Lion's Den Saloon on account of their
wives givin' her all their money, well she done up an' leave.
You never heared such cryin' an' carryin' on as them women
makes when they was biddin' her farewell an' not even noticin'
the big new autymobile she was drivin' or the fur coat she was
wearin'. She tell them ladies she get the call to go somewhere
else an' save more souls an' they all say she must go if she been
call. Ever one of them ladies is cryin' and actin' somethin'
awful not one of them seein' she done taken them for all they
got an' ever one of them is forgettin' when the spring run dry
you looks for another. The only place in town makin' more
noise than them ladies was Caney Church where you could
hear the hallaluin' for miles they was so happy to see her go.
Rev. Tatum say her leavin' bring more religion to Chickpea
than her comin' did an' now maybe he can get them women
folk back in the fold. But I low nobody is as sad to see her go

as Jerry Blumer who run the Lion's Den Saloon 'cause he know his business is goin' to take a slump.

Luke Porter's little boy, Dink, is sure growin' up an' is gettin' to be quite a handful for his parents. I remember when Dink was a little tot he give Luke an' Mary fits. One night the Porters has me over for dinner by mistake. I think I was invite 'cause Luke had somehow hear I was goin' to sell my house an' he want to list it for sale an' make a commission for himself. Anyway, that is beside the point. What I wants to tell you is that Dink refuse to eat his mash potatoes an' is almost drivin' his ma up the wall what with her tryin' to force them on him an' such. So I says to Mary, "Don't make Dink eat them mash potatoes 'cause they is grownups' food an' Dink is a baby." When Dink hear me say this he up an' say he ain't no baby an' he starts eatin' them mash potatoes like they is goin' out of style. Mary, she look at me real surprise like an' I just gives her one of my knowin' looks an' acts like I been handlin' kids all my life.

Everbody is complainin' these days. Mangus Stump was tellin' me how his wife waste a lot of money on clothes sayin' she want to be in style an' won't wear last year's dresses. But Mangus say the real reason is she get too fat. He say she is gettin' so expensive in her habits he is goin' to have to sell his chickens before they hatches.

I hope you is still thinkin' about comin' back to Chickpea when you retires. I bets you misses the smell of all that good food cookin' which is one of the best smells in a small town. Can't you just imagine walkin' down the street under them big elm trees an' smellin' all that bread bakin'?

Now, Elrod, I knows there is a lot of good folks in the city just like you writ an' tole me there is an' I'm sure you has a lot of good nabors an' such. But I lows most of them good folks in the city is folks what moves there from a small town. Anyways, I'm goin' to keep after you till you decides to come back here an' sleep in your old bed again.

That's all the news for now.

Cousin Hank

35

Chickpea
U.S.A.

Dear Cousin Elrod:

Us fellers was settin' down at the Cracker Barrel Gen. Store t'other day an' talkin' about the usual nonsense when somebody say it take two to argue an' of course Stew Borders have to put in his two cents worth an' he up an' low this ain't so an' go on to say his wife can do a real good job of arguin' all by herself an' when she do he can't get a word in at all an' there ain't no use of him tryin' to say nothin'.

An' then West Bennet show us some pineapples what has just been ship in from some islands he call Filipinos an' Mangus Stump say the first time he ever see a pineapple is right after he get back from World War One an' it like to of scairt him to death. He say he was afeared to touch it 'cause he think it is a hand grenade.

A friend of mine stop by on his way home from his vacation when he pass through Chickpea which I thinks is real nice of him. We goes to my kitchen to get us a cup of coffee an' this friend of mine happen to look out the window an' he cry out, "Look at that big rat!" This startle me 'cause I never has no rats before an' when I looks out the window I sees it ain't nothin' but a possum an' I am more than relieve. You know what, Elrod? That old possum start to hangin' around an' I been puttin' pieces of apple out on my back porch an' feedin' him just like he is a pet. An' you know somethin' else? T'other night I seen a raccoon eatin' on them apple pieces. Now that's somethin' you can't see or do in one of them big cities an' this is just one other thing I likes about a small town.

Incidentally, I might of eat that possum but it's like my friend say, it do look like a big rat.

I just can't understand folks, Elrod. Everybody is most upset when the County High School finish third in the basketball tournament 'cause they wants it to be first. But nobody seem to care when the news come out that the High School rank third from the bottom in the State when it come to eddycation.

Stew Borders get things mess up again. He been goin' around sayin' Miss Thornberry is hearin' voices. It seem she tole him the past speak to her through her books. Like I writ you before, he would get himself sue if he have anythin' worth suin' for.

We was talkin' t'other day down at the Cracker Barrel Gen. Store an' some of the fellers was lowin' how nice it will be when the population of Chickpea increase an' we won't no longer be a small town what some folks pokes fun at. Mordecai Collier up an' say the only trouble with Chickpea gettin' bigger is that it will have more autymobile traffic an' when things gets crowded the City Council will start puttin' up parkin' meters on Main Street an' no U-turn signs an' such will be springin' up all over the place an' he low he don't like that. But Danny Mings an' some others says this is progress an' that Chickpea can't stand still an' be a small town all its life. But Mordecai say that is just the point. Chickpea is a small town an' have all the charm of a small town an' all this will be lost if it get too big. Somebody else say if Chickpea get real big it will get a lot of bright street lights like you sees in the big city an' then you won't be able to see the stars unless you goes out of town. Mangus Stump say the bright lights will keep down crime. But Mordecai say Chickpea ain't got no crime an' Mangus say it will if it get bigger. An' Henry Ambrose say all this growth they is talkin' about will lead to one-way streets like Central City already have. This argument go back an' forth until I settles it by remarkin' taxes will go up, too. An' then everbody is satisfy with Chickpea the way it is.

I was standin' on the corner with Stew Borders an' Mangus Stump when Danny Mings walk up an' ask Stew to loan him twenty dollars. Stew say he ain't got twenty dollars on him but he will loan him ten dollars an' he hand Danny a ten-dollar bill. Danny thank him an' then say, "You now owes me

ten dollars an' that makes us even." An' he walk off leavin'
Stew standing' there with a real funny look on his face.
Mangus tell him, "Now that you done give him ten dollars
you won't see him no more an' I think you get off cheap."
Stew is a big loudmouth an' think he is the only person in
Chickpea who amount to anything. He think he is real big but
he ain't very tall an' don't weigh much. The only thing he can
do that nobody else can is read his own handwritin'. Walt
Blackton once say of him if he walk in a room full of people
you thinks somebody leave. Of course Stew won't agree to
this opinion we has of him. The only person Stew Borders
really have trouble with is Stew Borders.

That's all the news for now.

Cousin Hank

36

Chickpea
U.S.A.

Dear Cousin Elrod:

I'm tellin' you, Elrod, I'm goin' to keep on tryin' to get you
to come back to Chickpea when you retires. Don't you remember how quiet an' peaceful it is here? An' don't you
remember them big old houses we got here with them big
comfortable rooms? They was made for doin' a heap of livin'
in. They ain't like them little boxes what city folks lives in
with them rooms so small I heared you has to go outside to
change your mind. An' can't you just smell them leaves
burnin' in the fall? In Chickpea you can still burn them
without bein' afeared of gettin' arrested for breakin' the law.
An' if your feet hurts you can take off your shoes an' walk
around without some smart aleck askin' if you is from Kentucky. If you asks me it is them city fellers what is the real
hicks. We country folks learns more in a year watchin' what
go on in the barnyard than city folks learns in a lifetime of
readin' books.

You has just got to come back for your sake as well as mine 'cause you is the only relative I got left an' I sure has miss you a lot these many years. Just think how you can relax an' let your hair down if you ain't gone complete ball headed yet an' is wearin' a teepee on top of your head. Please let me know real soon what you is plannin' on doin' 'cause the waitin' for you to make up your mind is just about drive me out of mine. I just can't wait till we gets up in the mornin' an' I can say to you, "I reckon we ought to go over yonder to Coon Creek 'cause it look like the fish is goin' to be bitin' today." Remember how we use to catch them pan-size fish an' Ma would cook them with corn pone? That's the sweetest eatin' there is, Elrod, an' we ain't got that much time left so let's don't miss any more of it than we has to.

Not to be changin' the subject, but them fellers down at the Cracker Barrel Gen. Store sure can get themselfs in the dumbest arguments. Just yesterday they gets to talkin' about what they is raisin' an' Jake Staples he up an low he never raise no tobacco 'cause he ain't about to be sellin' no cancer. Now, Elrod, I knows the real reason he don't raise no tobacco is 'cause it take too much work an' he is like Stew Borders in that respeck bein' he is too lazy to do all the work it require. They both is nothin' but lazybodies an' to them ever day is the seventh day an' they rests. When Jake make this remark about not raisin' no tobacco Steve Weller tell him, "You feels that way 'cause you don't smoke. An' besides you is sellin' all that collessterall stuff when you takes your cattle an' hogs an' eggs to market an' that kill as many people as tobacco do accordin' to the experts." All this talk make West Bennet who run the Cracker Barrel Gen. Store most nervous on account of he make a lot of money sellin' such things as beef an' bacon an' eggs an' tobacco an' such an' he get in the conversation just to change the subject. Them fellers never seems to learn nothin' an' they will be arguin' the same thing next week. I remembers my pa quotin' that Plato feller who say you can't teach a old dog new tricks. I also hear he say you is never too old to learn an' I likes that one best.

That Doc Storkbill sure is a smart rabbit. He has been treatin' Henry Estes who is a retire teacher an' has been lookin' peaked for some time an' he wasn't gettin' nowhere with him. Doc tole me all Henry really need is exercise an' for a year he has been tryin' to get him to do a lot of walkin' but Henry won't do it. So Doc tole me he try some of his sycology on Henry an' tole him the only thing that will cure him is to eat a lot of morels which is a kind of mushroom that don't look at all like one of them toadstools which kill you if you eats it by mistake, or even if you eats it on purpose. Doc tole Henry you can't buy morels an' ever now an' then Henry find one an' take it home an' cook it an' eat it an' pretty soon he is lookin' real good again an' feelin' real spry like his old self. In fack, he look so good after awhile that Doc's son who is a undertaker begin to look real disappointed. Henry is real happy an' he tole Doc them morels is good medicine an' cure him, but Doc an' I knows it is the walkin' what do the curin'.

Stew Borders say he ain't superstitious but he do believe in luck 'cause if his nabors didn't have all the good luck an' him have all the bad luck they wouldn't be so much better off than him. I didn't want to make him feel bad or I would of tole him it is the feller what work hard what have the good luck. But I has to admit in farmin' if there is a drought or somethin' no matter how hard you works you has bad luck.

That's all the news for now.

Cousin Hank

P.S. How long's it been since you rested under a tree without settin' on a bench?

37

Chickpea
U.S.A.

Dear Cousin Elrod:

Ever since Otto Nelson die Chickpea don't have no town drunk. It bein' so unusual for a small town not to have a town drunk I won't be surprise if Chickpea don't show up in one of them books call World Records. I remembers once when some of us was tryin' to get Otto to straighten up an' quit drinkin' we taken him over one night to the distillery at Central City an' shows him all the lights lit up in them windows an' tells him they is makin' it fastern he can drink it. Otto, he stare at them lighted windows a spell an' then he say, "But I got them workin' nights."

Miss Pinwhistle an' Stew Borders both talks a lot an' they also talks fast, too. When they gets goin' good, Elrod, they talks a mile a minute with gusts up to five miles.

I meets Stew Borders an' he look so down I tries to cheer him up by tellin' him some feller I knowed tole me he was level headed, only I don't tell him the word this feller use was flat.

When you moves back here, as I'm hopin' you does, after you retires, you will enjoy knowin' Paul Milton who live down the street a piece. He move here about five year ago after retirin' from bein' a hardware man in Central City. He is one of the nicest fellers I ever knows an' is as clean as a hound's tooth.

Craig Jamison has gone an' got himself a girl friend. He is callin' on the Gilmore's an' takin out their daughter, Florabelle, quite a lot. I think he is gettin' serious 'cause I sees he's pettin' the cow to catch the calf an' is always takin' somethin' nice to Mrs. Gilmore evertime he call.

Kelly Vance give his annual barn dance last week an' invite a lot of folks he knows. If he just invite his friends there wouldn't have been so many at the dance. It's like Rev.

Tatum tole me, "If you has one friend, you is lucky." Anyways, there is a lot of fun in that old barn that night what with all the square dancin' an' such an' good fiddlin' by Hans Kruger who never have a lesson in his life but who play so you can tell what tune he is playin'. It's the first music I hears for a long time what don't have a guitar player an' it was a real relief. Them folks all dances real nice an' respeckful like an' not like them younguns today. I seen some of them younguns dancin' over to Central City once an' they reminds me of the time I watches a feller what is bein' stung by a lot of bees.

I asks Doc Storkbill why he don't try some of his sycology on Stew Borders who is always imaginin' he is sick, or got somethin' wrong with him, when he ain't. Doc say he do once but it don't work. He say he tole Stew he only feel bad 'cause he thinks he do an' if he would imagine he feel good he would feel good. But he say Stew tole him there is only one way to feel good an' over a hunerd ways to imagine you feels bad an' them odds is too much against him. Doc tole me he once think of chargin' Stew a big fee which he know has cure a lot of hippocondracks, but he give up the idea when he realize it would be just one more thing for Stew to worry about. So he tole me he decide to go on easin' Stew's mind in what he call a periodic pattern, which I think sound real important an' ought to work.

That's all the news for now.

Cousin Hank

38

Chickpea
U.S.A.

Dear Cousin Elrod:

Do you ever think how livin' in a small town is a eddyca-tion an' what it really mean to be borned an' raise in a small town? You learns one of the basic things in life an' that is how to get along with folks 'cause in a small town you has friends an' not just folks you knows, which is call acquaintances. An' while some of them gets on your nerves most of them doesn't. An' look how many of them famous folks comes from a small town or from the country near a small town. Do you ever refleck on how many presidents an' such was borned in a log cabin which is somethin' you don't see much of any more since the country growed an' they has cut down most of the trees an' makes boards out of 'em? You is always writin' me how busy folks is in the big cities. It look to me like you all is too busy to do much real livin'. You goes to college to get a degree or two so's you can make a lot of money an' you ends up with a nervous breakup. I knows a small town ain't for everone, Elrod, an' some folks even tole me they would go nuts livin' in a small town. I feel sorry for them 'cause they is the ones what has to be entertain all the time 'cause they don't know how to entertain theyselfs. I thinks maybe it is 'cause they gets too far from nature an' folks ain't ready for that yet. Like I says, in a small town you not only gets to learn a lot about folks but you learns a lot from them, too. You learns how to act an' behave by watchin' somebody what has got character like Mr. Estes, the retire school teacher who always set a good example even if he ain't make a lot of money. An' you can learn how not to act by watchin' a feller like Stew Borders who usually carry on like a idiot. An' even Miss Thornberry is somebody to look up to even if she do talk a lot. Whatever she tell you about yourself she mean for your own good. In the city you probably don't even know the name of the folks who lives next door to you an' I thinks that is kinda sad although I hears some folks say you is better off not knowin' your nabors an' I thinks that is kinda sad, too.

I knows you is wonderin' why I am writin' all this to you an' I has to confess it's to get you to come back here when you retires. I just wants you to know what you is missin'.

That's all the news for now.

Cousin Hank

39

Chickpea
U.S.A.

Dear Cousin Elrod:

We was talkin' down at the Cracker Barrel Gen. Store about sad things such as trouble an' such an' Henry Estes who has read a lot of what he call philosophy books an' has also been sad a lot tole us he get along real well laughin' at his troubles an' get rid of them that way. Stew Borders who ain't read hardly any books up an' low if he laugh at his troubles he would be in danger of laughin' himself to death. But Stew must of read somethin' now an' then 'cause he up an' say right surprisin' things once in a while, like the time he tole us he read somewhere where men is borned free. He go on to say he was borned free but then he get married. As you knows, Elrod, I likes to read too an' I read once if a man talk a lot he ain't got time to get into trouble, but this ain't so 'cause Stew Borders talk a lot an' the more he talk the more trouble he get into.

I writ you already about Koko sellin' a nostrum what is mostly alcohol an' is bought by folks who believes drinkin' is a sin. Well, Koko has come out with a new nostrum what he claim is a reducin' nostrum. I guesses he want to make money out of this dietin' fad what is goin' around an' finally reach Chickpea. Miss Pinwhistle who is already so thin she have to stand in the same place twice to throw a shadow go see Koko an' buy some of his nostrum what she think will help her keep her figger which I think could be improve on by her puttin' on a few pounds if she put them on in the right places. Anyways, after she pay for the nostrum she asks Koko if it really work an' he say, "It sure do. It already reduce your pocketbook."

The folks at Caney Church was talkin' about the church building havin' perfect acoustics which mean you can hear everthin' real good, an' Stew Borders, who fool me by knowin' what a acoustic is, say his idea of perfect acoustics is where you can't hear nothin'.

We was talkin' about buyin' on credit an' how it get folks in trouble when they spends more than they is able to pay for. Henry Ambrose say when he see all these folks spendin' their money makin' them monthly payments he is glad he buy everthin' he need by payin' all down an' nothin' a month. Doc Storkbill hear Henry say this an' he say he do a lot of his curin' on credit except when he get pay in things like tomatoes an' parsnips an' such outen folks' gardens. He go on to say the best collection agent he have to get folks to pay him what they owes him is when they gets sick again an' wants to make sure he take care of them.

Koko is lookin' real sad t'other day an' I asks him what is the matter an' he say he been thinkin' a lot since he read about man goin' out into space an' he feel real sorry for folks out there if man ever get hold of them 'cause look what he done to the Indians an' the buffalo an' such when he get hold of them.

Stew Borders tole us that when he go to the big city an' go to the movin' pitcher show house he get in without payin' by walkin' in backwards. He say they thinks he is comin' out an' don't ask him for a ticket.

Rev. Tatum give a sermon last Sunday on the sins of omission an' Henry Ambrose, who don't get to church on account of he drink too much Saturday night, ask Stew Border what sins of omissions is an' Stew low he ain't real sure but he thinks they is sins you should have commit but didn't.

You know, Elrod, it don't take no detecktiff to tell who is been buyin' moonshine from Lum Keller. All his customers has got sore spots on their noses from drinkin' out of mason jars.

That's all the news for now.

Cousin Hank

40

Chickpea
U.S.A.

Dear Cousin Elrod:
We was settin' an' spittin' down at West Bennet's Cracker Barrel Gen. Store which you may recall he also call the Federal Building since he rent out a room to the govment to sell stamps an' pick up mail an' such when somebody remark how quick we gets old. Mr. Estes, the retire school teacher, nod his head real wiselike an' say something none of us understand. Henry Ambrose up an' ask him, "What was that you say?" Mr. Estes repeat himself an' say, "Tempus Fugit." Of course this don't mean nothin' to Henry Ambrose or to any of us for that matter so Henry ask him what do it mean. Mr. Estes tole him it mean "time fly" an' is Latin what is a language spoken many years ago by folks who call theyselfs Romans. He go on to say it is a dead language. When he say this Henry ask him, "What kill it?" Henry say he don't rightly know but he thinks it must of die of old age. Pat Wilburn up an' low maybe there was a lot of Stew Borders among them Romans who talk so much they works it to death.

Stew Borders an' me goes to the Good Samaritan Hospital to see Miss Thornberry who Doc Storkbill has put in the hospital after she have a slight spell of somethin' which turn out not to be serious. While we is there a nice lookin' nurse come in wearin' a white cap what have a black band on it an' tole us Miss Thornberry has hire her to stay with her at night. Stew Borders ask her, "What do that cap on your head mean?" She tole him it show she is a registered nurse. On the way home Stew ask me if this mean she can vote an' I thinks this is one of the dumbest things he ever ask me. Anyways, when this nurse come in she look at all the flowers Miss Thornberry get 'cause she is a nice lady an' has got a lot of friends. When this nurse say to Miss Thornberry, "You sure do have a roomful of pretty flowers," Stew up an' low, "She couldn't have done better if she die." We asks Miss Thornberry how come Doc puts her in the hospital an' she say she get worried when she see spots before her eyes an' Stew ask her if she seen a doctor an' she say, "No, just spots." Before I can get Stew out of there he get to talkin' a lot as usual an' he tole us when he was in the hospital he had a practical nurse what taken care of him an' he low she must have been call a practical nurse on account she marry a rich old man who was a patient down the hall.

Mr. Estes tole us he use his imagination a lot 'cause he ain't got the money to do everthin' he want to so he just imagine he do things. He say he enjoy doin' this an' in some ways thinkin' about somethin' is better than doin' it especially thinkin' about them things what can get you in trouble. I asks him why he don't use all this imagination he got an' write a book an' he tole me he think about that a long time ago an' start writin' a book but in ten years all he has got writ is the title an' now he is beginnin' to get discourage. Mr. Estes entertain us a lot tellin' us about things what happen in the past an' some of them is just awful like what folks does to each other before they gets enlighten an' even after they gets enlighten. He scare some of us when he say history repeat an' none of us wants to be around if it do. Some of us thinks things is bad enough they way they is an' we don't want history comin' back an' messin' things up worsern they is.

That's all the news for now.

Cousin Hank

41

Chickpea
U.S.A.

Dear Cousin Elrod:
   You has done make me very happy tellin' me you is comin' back here to live an' I can't hardly wait to meet you when you gets off the plane in Central City next week. I am goin' to miss writin' to you but havin' you here is goin' to make up for it an' for all the years you has been away.
   Just let me know the exact time you're gettin' in to Central City an' your old Cousin Hank will be there to meet you.
   I'm savin all the news till you gets here.

Cousin Hank